THE PRISONER

Falling Run Press

THE PRISONER

By:

Michael Cary

"The right method of philosophy would be this. To say nothing except what can be said, *i.e.* the propositions of natural science, *i.e.* something that has nothing to do with philosophy: and then always, when someone else wished to say something metaphysical, to demonstrate to him that he had given no meaning to certain signs in his propositions. This method would be unsatisfying to the other – he would not have the feeling that he were teaching him philosophy – but it would be the only strictly correct method."

"My propositions are elucidatory in this way: he who understands me finally recognizes them as senseless, when he has climbed out through them, on them, over them. (He must so to speak throw away the ladder, after he has climbed up on it.)"

"Whereof one cannot speak, thereof one must be silent."

--Ludwig Wittgenstein, the final three propositions in his *Tractatus Logico-Philosophicus*

The Prisoner

"Where the fuck is my drink? I thought I asked you to get it for me half an hour ago."

"Sorry Estel," said Edna. "I'll fetch one now."

"Finally," was all that was said as he reached across the bed for the small wooden cup of wine poured by Humbert.

After a few sips, each of which preceded a menacing yet almost furtive glance at the cup, as though it was in the wrong and it knew that it was so yet had no intention of belying this fact, he broke his own short lived silence, uttering without altering the disapproving grimace from his face, "This is disgusting."

"Sorry Estel, it was the best I could make and you know that they don't allow for alcohol to be brought into our community and this is the best I could make." Humbert cringed and wrung his hands as the words left his mouth, deeply worried as he had been ever since the first sip of his in house sangria was taken.

"Try harder next time."

"What's going on? Who are you two and how did you get here?" The line from Joseph was stated with the tone which one typically assumes when they are guising the near certainty they have for their own answer to the conundrum at hand in case they are wrong, as if he knew these people intimately from some past, unrecallable life.

"Damn it Joseph, you never make anything easy."

"That's right, you're Estel. You're the one that made me move into the community."

"I suppose you could say that."

"You suppose?" The pleasant smirk that had been subtly dominating Joseph's countenance gave way to a more concerted expression, an expression which only intensified when he saw the utter indifference across the entire body of the man sitting on his bed. "Are you insinuating that this is by some means my fault?"

"Fault? Now that is interesting…"

"That's not what I meant. Is that my cup of wine sitting next to you?" The nod in response prompted another question. "Would you hand it here please? Thank you." The cup was passed from one hand to the other. "Thanks."

With only one man sitting on the bed, the rays from the sun began to creep in through the window, leaving an inverted image of the small lone window of the room growing across the floor. "The stripes are beautiful, so delicate and tender," said Humbert. The tantalizingly mildness of the soft inversion had absolutely riveted him, reminding him of someone of whom he once knew intimately.

"You would." The words of Estel echoed gruffly across the room. "Go away, you aren't wanted here anyways."

"That reminds me, I have to meet the preacher tonight," declared Joseph. "I had better get some sleep."

"I think I will too," came timidly from the mouth of Humbert. "Yes, it is probably for the best anyways."

Finding himself alone in the room for the first time in a while, Estel noticed that he had the perfect opportunity to reflect on what he knew the day would all too soon bring. It certainly was not going to be pleasant, perhaps the worst experience of his life, but after all this was why he had joined the community in the first place.

On the lone bed in the room he shifted into a new position at the end of the mattress nearest the window in order to avoid the corner of the inverted portrait of the window created by the sunlight that had begun to creep onto the far corner of the bed and more significantly its accompanying warmth, and enjoyed the rare luxury of silent aloneness that had momentarily presented itself. The whininess of Humbert, a man who longed for a long past time in his life, was incredibly frustrating, though now harmless enough. But the inquisitiveness that was rapidly developing within Joseph was proving troublesome. Joseph was slowly gaining an alarming degree of awareness of the actions and goings-on in their portion of the community, an awareness which Estel knew would lead to a realization that Joseph could never handle.

Just then Edna appeared. "Hey dear, how are you?"

The only response she garnered was a meek yet characteristically gruff grunt.

"Well then..." Her voice trailed off as she struggled to summon the courage to say what she so desperately wanted to say to him. After a deep sigh, "You look like you need to talk." A short pause ensued during which Estel slowly raised his head to make eye contact with Edna, as though the sincerity of her words could manipulate even his actions. "What's on your mind sweetheart?"

After a letting out a sigh of his own, Estel began to recount his latest interaction with Joseph. "He now knows that he belongs here."

"Oh, I see..." Her voice trailed off as before. "Well, does he know where here is?"

"Not yet, at least not as far as I can tell. But I'm worried that he might uncover a little more, what with the importance of today, and even the most trivial recollection, the slightest bit more knowledge, could bring forth a cascade of memories which we could never control." He paused before stating even more sternly, "This could be the end for us."

"I see. What should we do about him?"

"He's asleep right now. First we keep it that way as long as we can. Second we feed him what's left of the wine and distract him with meaningless banter until the time comes."

"Do you really think that will work?"

"We would have to be careful, making sure that nothing we say could possibly be construed into something meaningful." Estel shot a vicious look at Edna.

"Okay, I suppose we can try... Oh I just wish he hadn't just begun to come around here at the very end." Her tone was worried with a subtly desperate underscore of the inevitability of failure.

"Just let me handle this situation, and if you can, avoid talking to him at all. Whatever you do, don't, I repeat don't, let him know what you are thinking."

"Okay, I'll try my best." Yet again one of her statements garnered only a grunt, this one rather vocal in the discontent of its maker.

"Well, what do we do now until he wakes up?" Being that the two were both on the bed, Estel forcibly grasped Edna's hand and placed it over the front of his pants. She felt within the grasp of her hand something growing. As it grew she released it and not so reluctantly drove her hand into the front of his pants just as forcefully as he had grabbed her by the wrist only moments earlier. When she reached his penis, she gave it a quick, teasing tug before completely removing his pants. Before returning, however, she furtively looked around the room for some sort of lubrication, but in their Spartan barracks none was to be found. She did not want to spit in her hand; the faint, unpleasant smell would linger for the rest of the day, reminding her of the disgusting deed incessantly.

With no other options she followed through with the degrading act which she regretted before performing it. The warmth of the spit on his penis instantly relaxed Estel, converting his gruff grunts into smooth, baritone enunciations of ecstasy. After a few minutes the deed was done. Her hand was covered in an even more disgusting bodily fluid than before, and with no running water she came to a horrendous realization, namely that she had to find somewhere where she could clean her hand as thoroughly as possible. Unfortunately this would at best amount to finding an absorbent surface on which she could wipe her hand. Looking around at her surroundings, the bed was the only viable option. She wiped her hand thoroughly across the thin blanket serving as a comforter, inspecting her hand upon completion, her hopes lifting as she noted that it visibly appeared clean, but after a cursory sniff of the stench which would linger for the rest of the day, her dejection was complete.

Sinking back into the wall serving as a headboard, Estel reached to pull his pants back around his waist. When his upper back just below his neck first hit the concrete he awkwardly thrust his hips forward, perfectly straightening his back from his hips to his shoulders, so that his pants could return to their proper place, secured around his waist.

"Of course those two are curled up sleeping together in the bed." The passing remark went unnoticed by the self-absorbed companions, at least until they noticed that it had awoken Joseph.

"Ah, what a refreshing sleep. What time is it?" Joseph sat up in the bed and looked around the room for a clock, noticing that he was entirely alone. There was, however, a faint smell emanating from his bed, a familiar smell which he could not quite place. Ignoring it, he began to try to remember what had been on his mind before he went to bed so long ago. He hazily recalled something about a man in important garb. The images slowly etched onto the inner surface of his mind their own intricacies until he remembered his meeting that evening with the preacher. He wondered what it may be about. For some reason it weighed heavily on his mind, yet he could not quite place the purpose of their impending conversation.

He attempted to rid himself of his nagging suspicion that it would not go well for him. "Hopefully that is not foreboding in any way," he said aloud.

"What's that?" asked Estel.

"I just remembered that meeting tonight with the preacher, but for some reason I have this feeling that it isn't going to go too well for me."

"Don't worry about it. Here, finish your drink from earlier." Again the drink was passed from the same right hand to the same left hand as before.

After taking a large sip Joseph stared into his cup inquiringly. "This is terribly strong for a sangria."

"Good, so finish it." Joseph begrudgingly obliged, emptying the cup. "Here, have some more. You look like you could use it."

The severity of his tone initially proved efficacious as Joseph willingly continued to drink. But as he finished the second cup he began to grow talkative. While Estel was pouring an unannounced third cup of the wine which went through its fermentation process in the very room in which the two men now stood his concentration shifted temporarily from Joseph to the wine. Though he did not spill any of the wine, he did proffer an opportunity for Joseph to begin to debate with himself unobserved the austerity of the room.

"Why is this room so very terrible? The bed is too firm and the sheets are too thin, the room is cold and these cement walls only exacerbate the chill I feel, in fact, the only thing keeping the ice from freezing me to my very marrow is the strength of that terrible wine. Who would live here anyways?"

Estel felt his eyes dilate, but keeping his head down, facing only the now full cup of wine, he feared Joseph may presently be embarking on the very path from which he was obligated to prevent Joseph from ever finding.

"Wait a minute... You live here, don't you?" Uncertain of how he should respond at this sudden lunge towards a possible undesirable clarity, Estel paused for just too long to prevent Joseph from continuing. "I'm sorry, I didn't mean to be rude. I know it isn't the best of accommodations, but none of them are that great here at the community, are they? In fact, this bed looks exactly like mine... Wait, we're in my room aren't we? Oh lord, I'm sorry. My mind must have been too preoccupied by my meeting with the preacher tonight. I was planning on going to visit you to talk about it anyways, and, well, seeing you here... Never mind, I'm sorry."

Estel calculated the odds of stopping the personal enlightenment unfolding before his eyes. Ultimately he decided to sacrifice what was already too apparent for the opportunity to instantiate the counter attack brewing in his mind, a byproduct of the many games of chess he had played in his spare time since joining the community.

"Don't fret over it." A reluctant sigh he let out as he realized what must come next. "Why don't we talk about something more lighthearted until you have to leave, you know, to ease the stress?" The assistance he offered was humiliating humble, though Estel knew that the indignity he must suffer would be for the best provided the short time he likely had left to live.

"You know, Estel, these people here bother me ever so much. You I know well after all, but the others… Edna and Humbert are sufferable, though I suspect that they are hiding something from me; nothing anyone says is ever what they mean in this place, but everyone else, those strangers, they are absolutely abominable. In fact, every time I see one of the others I feel as though something is inherently wrong about this community which you have led me to."

"Joseph!" An immediate interruption intuitively felt indispensable given the direction in which his cohort was directing the conversation. "The community is where you belong. These people are the closest friends you have. This place is everything to you right now. Besides, you didn't even sleep that long, maybe you should try taking another nap."

Joseph felt himself instantly become heavy-eyed and lethargic, but he had one last reality to establish before he went to sleep. "Thank you, roommate. Your perspicacity is both immeasurably practical and greatly welcomed." With that line uttered Joseph disappeared into a deep slumber.

"Finally," Estel brusquely stated in relief.

"Finally what?" asked Edna who had appeared just as Joseph fell asleep.

"He's getting closer to the truth. Just before he departed he called me his roommate. And to think, he was unaware for so long, through so many tribulations we kept this from him, and now, on the most inopportune of days, he begins to piece it all together. He must have heard something from somewhere, somehow."

"The truth is hard to find." Edna innocently pressed forward the conversation, "What did he have to say of Humbert and I?"

"He has made the first step."

Edna stared back at him in astonishment as the many fears of old raced through her mind. If she were to be found out she would be directly responsible for the demise of everyone. And though she must remain calm, an unnerving task with this new revelation, she at least had the time necessary to regain her composure since Joseph was not around.

Just then two guards approached Joseph's room. One standing alert as the other opened the door, the first guard called out, "Joseph, are you in there?"

The second guard shot the first a brief look of disbelieving compunction. "Should you really be doing that?" he whispered without any deviation of his eyes from the door.

Before any retort could be made, however, a falsetto sang across the room, "He's sleeping right now, can you come back later?"

"No," replied the first guard. "We need him to come out now."

The second guard, finally allowing his eyes to break contact with the door for the most diminutive of moments, turned his head towards his counterpart and rolled his eyes in disgust at the decision just made before returning his gaze to a fixed one on the door.

After an eerily long silence leaching from the open doorway, the first guard had set his mind to making the demand again when a gruff brusquerie caught him by surprise, startling him even.

"I don't know why you two are still here; Joseph is in no position to come out right now."

"Oh, you..." The tone of the voice of the first guard was noticeably worried, a sentiment obviously shared by the second guard whose countenance so distinctly displayed a similar startling. Estel had never before responded on behalf of Joseph as this was a task usually appointed to Edna who loved the attention it offered, thus the guards were uncertain as to how they should proceed.

"Well, you of all people certainly know why we are here." The second guard had knowingly spoken out of turn and tried to guise this fact with an overt irritation in his tone, but the first guard, and more importantly Estel, knew that he was in the wrong.

"Look, leave Joseph alone. He isn't due to meet the preacher for quite a while yet, and trust me, you don't want to deal with what you are going to invoke."

"We're not here to take him to the preacher. He needs to clarify some of the final details of his stay with the specialist." The first guard forcefully took charge of the conversation from both Estel and his colleague.

"Again, you don't want to do this. I will take care of whatever this person needs on his behalf. How's that?"

Letting out an audible sigh, the first guard replied, "I don't have time for this. Just come with us. You know the process."

Estel, hands in the air and his pockets turned out, walked out of the room and towards the guards as slowly as his legs would permit. The first guard closed the door behind Estel and grabbed his arms, pinning them behind his back where they were handcuffed. Meanwhile the second guard began the task of shackling the ankles. As the chained and shackled man trudged his way down the narrow corridor overly lit with bright fluorescent lighting with the two guards flanking his either side, he could sense the many faces hiding behind the walls which all knew of his fate and pitied him immeasurably.

The long, slow walk ended at the desk which left barely enough room between the back of the chair which sat behind it and the brick wall that marked the end of the corridor and the building itself. The chair was facing the brick wall, but as the sound of the shuffling of the shackles stopped it swiveled around revealing a withered old face with a long, crooked nose sitting atop a thin mustache placed delicately on the top of the upper lip, all of which perfectly accented a large, though clean, mole in between the corner of the mustache and the outermost of the left nostril. "What would you like for your dinner tonight?"

"You mean what would Joseph want for dinner tonight?"

"Yes, I meant *Joseph*." If the initial tone was not patronizing enough, this last retort reeked of superiority.

"Well, knowing Joseph as well as I do..."

"Don't look at me when you speak! Stare at the desk." Estel, even in his shackled state, intimidated the

- 20 -

specialist, somehow managing to exude such confidence that the eye contact made was becoming physically painful to the man behind the desk.

Begrudgingly fulfilling the request, Estel began again, though careful to further enhance the tonal confidence of his voice so as not to lose control of the situation for his answer was of incredible importance. "*Well*, knowing Joseph as well as I do, I would say that he would be content so long as he isn't served something Mediterranean. Let's go with something hearty, French, perhaps a Potage Saint-Germain? Yes. Then lamb chops with rosemary and, how about, yes, a small garden salad to finish."

"And for dessert?"

"For desert anything will do so long as it isn't baklava."

"I'll make a note of it." Swiveling back around so that he was again facing the brick wall, he made a final demand, "Take him back to his room."

By the time Estel had successfully been unshackled, Edna, Humbert, and Joseph were all awaiting him in the room. Even though within his mind he was ruminating over the gamble which he had just made, he knew that he must empty himself of such thoughts to prevent Edna from allowing Joseph to uncover anything new. The man with whom he had just spoken was legally bound to adhere to any dinner requests, but that man was not to be trusted. To openly mention the significance of Mediterranean food and the importance of avoiding it ran the risk of being double crossed whereby Joseph would be fed the delectable dessert, but with others present he felt it a safer alternative than running the risk that baklava could be chosen as an arbitrary dessert to finish the course.

"Where were you?" The inquisitiveness of Joseph had returned along with his own self-awareness.

"Just helping to prepare dinner for us tonight. Forget it."

"No! What are we having? I would really like something sweet."

"Nothing sweet. You have to meet the preacher after dinner and eating sweets would be inappropriate."

"I understand," Joseph lied. He was craving something specific, but he could not quite place the name of the particular saccharine indulgence he had in mind. "But still, why were you preparing dinner for the four of us? Wouldn't dinner for two be more appropriate?" Then, switching to a whisper, "Besides, I don't trust those two. I don't even know who they are or why they insist on being in my room."

"You shouldn't trust them. In fact, if you forget about them I'd venture to guess they would disappear entirely."

"I wish it were that easy, but…"

"But it is," bullied its way into the conversation as a stern interjection from Estel.

"*But*… But I dearly want to figure out why they are here and who they are. So I think I shall." The power of that last jovially spoken line caused Estel to leave the room. Sitting on his bed, Joseph realized that the one of the two in question was sitting alongside him on the bed. "Who are you?"

The falsetto that warbled it way throughout the room seemed oddly familiar to him. "You really don't remember me?"

"Your voice sounds familiar, but I can't quite place where I first heard it. Nevertheless, you are always here in my room with me and seemingly following me everywhere I go. Why?"

"If you remembered me you would know why." The tone in her voice had shifted from that of a scolding mother to one indicative of a sad plea for attention. "Why can't you remember me Joseph?"

"I don't know. You're always here, always a nuisance, and I apparently am more concerned with your presence than who you are. If I knew why you lived in my room perhaps then I could learn who you are." Once the words which had just emanated from his mouth met his ears he realized the implication of his statement. "You are my roommate too!"

"Yes! Yes I am! But what about Humbert?"

"I suppose he is too, but he is the least present of the three of you.

"And why is that?"

"I don't know. I suppose it's because he reminds me of someone whom I once knew and didn't like very much."

"Well, you don't have to ignore him so much. You could learn more from him than you could ever imagine." She shuddered at these last words of hers; she had gotten carried away in the pleasantness of the discussion and given away to Joseph too much information. In fact, she regretted the entire conversation. It was all a mistake, a mistake which felt oddly forced from her by some unseen, outside force.

Just then Humbert appeared, taking the place of Edna.

"Oh, you're back I see," observed Joseph.

"Yes, yes I am." The response was shaky but delightful, full of some preoccupation. A family had just walked past the door to Joseph's room, a family comprised of a mother, a daughter of about twelve, and a toddler son struggling to keep up alongside the long strides of his mother whose hand he was holding. Humbert, stricken by the appearance of the young girl, left the bed and walked to the door where he stood and watched the family, or more precisely the daughter, walk out of sight down the corridor.

Returning to the bedside, Humbert decided to hide his motives from Joseph per the earlier demand of Estel. The task wasn't easy for him as was evident from the way he continuously shifted his glance across the room, but he nevertheless maintained his silence for long enough. Joseph, pleased with his progress, opted to take another nap.

Estel, taking advantage of Joseph's slumber, scolded Edna. "What did you just do? You told him far too much. Because of you he is going to uncover everything; because of you we are going to be slaughtered like cattle! Why would you do this?!" Then muttering to no one in particular, "All of my years of hard work is going to be ruined..."

"I'm sorry, Estel! I couldn't help it! It's not my fault, someone made me say that stuff to him, I swear!"

"I told you—"

"I'm sorry! What else can I say? I didn't mean it! I'm sorry Estel."

Sighing audile discontent, Estel turned his back on Edna. Standing before the window he began to plan how he could rectify Edna's mistake.

Several minutes had passed in silence when the guards came again. The same two from before assumed their previous positions and again called for Joseph. Edna was again the first to answer as Estel was still deep in thought and hesitated. "What do you want?"

"It's time for...*you* to shower."

"Okay, so I will go to the washroom. Open the door."

"Yes, yes you will, but we still have to escort you there."

"Why?"

"Those are the rules."

"But why are they the rules? It seems superfluous to me."

"For your own safety."

"But from whom would you be protecting me?"

"Yourself jackass, now get out here!" The second half of the sentence came in the form of a controlled, angry shout.

"You don't have to be so mean, you know." Edna slowly walked out of the room where she was forcibly cuffed and shackled by the two guards just as they had done less than an hour before. They ushered her in the opposite direction down the corridor from the desk adjacent the brick wall, in the same direction in which the family that she remembered had earlier drawn the attention of Humbert had passed. The reached an intersection with another corridor at which a left turn was made. The third door on the right led into the showers. They were entirely unoccupied at this time, a precaution made by the man who sat behind the desk. Edna was unshackled and told to undress. When her many requests for privacy all went unheeded she shyly obliged before being handed a simple bar of soap. Much to Edna's chagrin the guards never even turned away as she turned on the water and began to lather her body. Rather, they stared earnestly at her exposed, naked flesh. The experience was embarrassing, leading Edna to take control of the situation by rinsing the soapy bubbles off of her body as provocatively as possible and extending the shower for as long as possible. Toweling herself dry, Edna handed the slippery bar of soap to one of the guards who cautiously handed her a safety razor in return.

"What's this for?"

"To shave your face... Oh not this. If you don't think you need it, just hand it back." The first guard wanted nothing more than to end the awkwardness as quickly as possible.

Edna faced the guards and dropped the towel to the floor before turning around and slowly bending over, waiving her hips back and forth as she grabbed her clothes. After she had completed the sanitary requests made by the guards and redressed, she was shackled again for the trek back to Joseph's room.

"At least you almost look presentable now."

"Was this all really necessary, you two staring at my sexy, glistening, wet, naked body while I showered?"

The two guards simultaneously broke their gazes from Edna to look at each other awkwardly. Two silent nods in agreement were all Edna received.

Frustrated, Edna put a frown on her face and the journey back to the room proceeded in silence. Upon being unshackled yet again, she went back into the room.

Joseph greeted Edna after she entered the room. In an effort to avoid any conversation, Edna decided to leave.

Feeling surprisingly relaxed yet equally unrested all at once, an oddity considering how often he had been sleeping lately, Joseph decided to lie down in the bed and go to sleep. The instant the mildewed blanket atop his tattered sheets reached his chin he felt his eyes close and his mind start to empty when a sudden stench found his nose. It reeked of saliva and something else which he could not quite place. He examined the blanket, but in its decomposed state there were no obvious culprits to be found, rather only many possible malefactors, each as plausible as the next.

But when he repositioned the blanket snugly underneath of his chin, the odor returned. Upon one final examination he discovered that the smell was coming from his own hand, faintly, as if it were insufficiently masked by soap. "Odd," he thought aloud as he drifted into a deep sleep.

CHAPTER 2

A knock came upon his door, waking him from his sleep and rendering Joseph duly frightened. The two guards had returned.

When Joseph first awoke, still hypnopompic, he saw the young woman from his dreams. "Stop! You're going to kill me!" he screamed at the subreptitious shadow of the bedpost cast upon the wall before his vision could delineate the true image manifested before him and render him fully conscious.

"What are you yelling about now?" sighed the first guard.

"Nothing... Nothing," was the subservience offered by Joseph. He had a sneaking suspicion that the woman from his dream was going to be responsible for his death, but he also felt an inherent comfortable familiarity and safety with this woman. Confused and knowing that he needed more time to assimilate his perceptions of this young woman in order to discern who she was and what she meant to him, he hid his knowledge of this woman from the guards for fear that they might somehow take from him his knowledge of her.

"Well hurry up and put these on." The second guard threw a tattered suit through the still closed door towards Joseph while the first spoke his demand.

Much like the woman, Joseph felt the suit to be oddly familiar. But just as he was beginning to stuff his first leg through the waist of the pants Estel appeared, demanding from Joseph the suit so that he could don it himself. "Give it to me," he whispered, "and let me go in your stead." Though the phrasing was passive, there was only the utmost stipulation in his tone.

Estel, once dressed, walked to the door and said, "I'm ready."

"Oh god, here we go again..." The first guard dramatically rolled his eyes, ensuring that the man standing on the other side of the door could see this action. "At least *you* know how this works."

Chained and shackled, Estel was led by the two guards to the cafeteria. The room, as massive as it was, was entirely empty at this odd time in the late afternoon. It was too early for dinner by at least an hour, but lunch had come and passed many hours before. After being unchained and unshackled yet again by the guards Estel took a seat, taking the time to look around the vacant square and observe every familiar row of seating, every empty aisle, even the unoccupied territory typically claimed by the usual mealtime lines of hungry patrons from the community as he slowly lowered himself onto the bench.

"Don't you dare think about moving, Joseph."

"Estel."

"Right, *Estel*." The tone of the first guard returned to the patronizing timbre with which Estel had become all too accustomed.

Just then the double doors from the kitchen swung open and a man donning a chef's hat and an apron walked towards Estel carrying a large platter concealed by a dome shaped cover. He sat the platter before Estel and ornately removed the cover. Below lied a bowl of chicken and lemon rice soup garnished with dill with only a single spoon flanking the steaming metal bowl.

"You may eat." The words triggered a response from Joseph who had found his way into the cafeteria shortly after Estel had arrived.

"Isn't this supposed to be my dinner?"

"Yes, but it's for the best that I eat it this time. Especially considering this isn't what I ordered for you. Go away." Estel had yet to lose his calm either in tone or countenance, but underneath he was trembling with fear. His gamble had backfired; the man from behind the desk at the end of the corridor had intentionally sabotaged the dinner request Estel had made, serving the worst possible fare imaginable.

"No! You have always gotten your way! I have been waiting all day for this meal." Switching from an angry shout to a grateful whisper, "Thank you, by the way. This is *exactly* what I would have requested. You don't have to lie; you're a good friend." Then reverting back to his original disposition coupled with a healthy dose of sarcasm, "This meal is really important to me, so, *if you would please*, let me have this."

"No."

"Estel, give me my dinner."

"No."

"Estel, I said give me my dinner!"

"No."

Taking a deep breath and mimicking his counterpart in severity, "What exactly is it that you are trying to keep from me?"

"What could I possibly be hiding from you?"

"I know about the girl."

With that line Estel lost all strength and gave way to Joseph, and the man for whom the dinner was intended all along began his first course. He heard the voice of Estel in his ear, whispering an intrinsic plea of desperation for Joseph to abruptly stop. "You're going to regret this!" But when he looked down his soup was almost gone. He had just had his first mouthful, but the bowl was nearly empty. He wondered if Estel had eaten the rest without him knowing. Time had passed in an awkward leap forward, not permitting him the luxury of enjoying the most decadent meal he had been afforded in recent memory. This, he had noticed, had become an all too often occurrence in his life. His perception of time had been altered roughly when his sleeping habits had shifted such that he often found himself dozing in the middle of the day, sometimes sleeping for what felt like years on end.

As he was finishing the soup a gesture was made by the first guard towards the kitchen where from within emerged again the chef carrying a second platter.

But within his mind Joseph saw not the community chef, but the chef from his boarding school as a child. The memories poured into his mind, leaving the filter which was once so unporous a now precariously penetrable perviousness.

"Joseph! Stop!" again whispered scornfully inside of his head.

He could see the chef in vivid detail, chef's whites with an emblazoned blue and gold crest emblemizing the boarding school, carrying toward he and his friends the silver platter on which were as many small bowls of seafood stew as there were children, each meal garnished with its own basil leaf. His childhood progressed before his eyes. Every young boy whom he once knew to run about to and fro and every retrospectively laughably false rumor they once spread that had infiltrated his mind and consumed his personality had conjured themselves, blotting out the cafeteria of the community, replacing the real view with their fantastical, whimsical, delusional selves.

He was taken back to one day in particular. During the short walk by the chef from the kitchen double doors to the table at which Joseph was sitting, Joseph managed to replay the marquee events in an oneiromantic trance.

"Joseph!" The voice of a young boy rang out across the tranquil sea of clover, green broken by patches of white, and struck him as distinctly familiar though not quite incontrovertible in source. But as the shouting continued the young boy could be seen running into frame, trampling the clover as he approached. He was short and thin as young boys once were, clad in his school uniform of a solid dark blue with a blue and gold diagonally striped tie hanging entirely in front of his blazer from his recent exertion, hiding the gold buttons which adorned the blazer as it swung back and forth across his chest with each taken stride.

"Joseph!" Without hesitating to catch his breath, a luxurious corollary of his youthful fitness, he progressed to tell his tale. "Joseph! You must come see! Thomas found it over there!" The accompanying gesticulation indicated that the incredible find was located not a hundred meters out of frame, near the woods line which marked the edge of campus.

"What is it Max?!" protested Joseph as he ran stride for stride with his classmate towards the foliage. Upon arrival his question was immediately answered; the lacy pink cloth was lying soiled upon the ground in the most erotic display imaginable at such an age. Of the half dozen boys clamored around the prize finding, all but Joseph had managed to find themselves a girlfriend at the school across the street, many of whom had even managed to win their first kiss. The humiliation which Joseph endured on a daily basis from his friends burned inside him once again, causing him to snatch the lingerie from the ground and run as fast as he could away from the other boys.

The chase was intense; Joseph felt his lungs burning, screaming for oxygen, as he fought hard to maintain the lead he had gained from his unanticipated action. Covering the first kilometer in barely over three minutes, Joseph turned around in time to watch the last of his friends quit their pursuit. He was now clear across the campus, near the front door to the dormitory, so he decided to go sneak into his room. After darting across the front lawn and shutting the door behind himself, Joseph monitored his breathing and began to climb the staircase. He ensured that each step he took was as surreptitious as the last so as to prevent anyone who may be lurking in the building from discovering his treasure, yet hastened the ascent as quickly as silence would allow.

Once he was up the stairs and into his shared room, he locked himself in the bathroom. Uncertain of his own impending action, though aware of its imminence, his hands began to tremble as he removed his blazer and placed it upon the counter. Next came his tie, though the process of untying it took nearly a full minute as the trembling of his hands had progressed to a readily visible shaking and he continuously fumbled the tie every which way but loose. After his tie joined his blazer next to the sink, he reached for the top button on his shirt. Feeling at this point that he was fully committed to the sin, his breathing had become quick, short, and shallow. The diminutive amount of oxygen he was receiving exacerbated the intensified need for the self-compounded element he had from his earlier escape and left him feeling dizzy. He had also began to sweat lightly about his collar and from the bottom of the neatly kempt hairline on the back of his neck. The button was stubborn, but once it was unbuttoned he began the decent down his chest and each button became easier than the last. With his shirt unbuttoned he thrust it at the counter, a bit too enthusiastically, causing it to land in the empty sink. Not paying any attention to where his shirt had landed, Joseph kicked off his shoes and pants as quickly as he could and stared at his prize.

The age of eleven, being as difficult and tumultuous of a time in the life of a boy as it is, comes with many odd feeling and an accompanying exploration of the body. Joseph stood there naked, staring at his reflection in the mirror as he began to touch himself. His hands ran across his chest where his nipples evinced a heightened sensitivity to contact. Evoking within him an unknowingly sexual frenzy, Joseph moved his hands to his back and slowly let them sink towards his buttocks. Once there they quickly ceased sensually caressing the skin and began grabbing and slapping, though he knew not why.

Next came his penis. For some reason it stood erect, and upon contact with his hand exhibited a sensitivity so heightened from the norm that it induced the first deep breath he had taken in minutes. The surprise and awe from this scintillating sensation and the relief from the oxygen caused him to let go of himself and press himself against the edge of the counter. Again he knew not why he did what he did, but it was honest and instinctual. The counter, however, was frigid and caused him to jump back as a shocked response.

All of these newfound phallic feelings were deeply confusing as he knew not why any of them were occurring or what they meant. None of the other boys talked about any of this, and all of the other boys had girlfriends. Joseph found himself wandering if what he was doing was not just morally wrong, but unforgivable and indicative of there being something seriously wrong with his masculinity. Taking another deep breath, Joseph began to do precisely what he had intended to do all along.

In his hand he clutched the lace enveloped pink piece of lingerie and stepped into it. Pulling it up to his waist, he found that it was actually small enough to fit around him, even using it to press his penis perfectly upright against his lower abdomen. Then, pulling the connected brassiere upward, he held it in place in front of his chest. The straps dangled at his sides, and try as he might, he could not manage to hook them together behind his back. He let go of the top and let it drape to his knees. Sitting down on the closed toilet lid, he hooked the straps together before standing back up. From there it was only a matter of leaning forward and contorting his torso in various directions to get the lingerie in its proper place.

Again he admired himself in the mirror, now more confused and guilt-ridden than ever. He cupped his 'breasts' in his hands, pushing them up while lightly squeezing them. He admired his flat stomach striped with the long, thin strands of taut pink lace that connected the top to the bottom. He saw in the mirror something more a young woman and less a young man. He wondered if perhaps the reason that he was the only one of his friends yet to sustain a relationship with a girlfriend, to treasure his first kiss with a young girl, was that he was not meant to ever have a girlfriend. It was only fitting, then, that he should be wearing an extravagant piece of lingerie in that moment. It was only fitting, then, he felt so embarrassed. It was only fitting, then, that he should not be normal.

But just then, at the most inopportune of moments, shouting was faintly discernible from the common room as his friends raced towards the bathroom door. As they approached the door Joseph panicked, checking and double-checking that the door was locked before he began to hastily remove the piece from his body, accidentally tearing it in twain. Even with the other boys now pounding on the door, all Joseph could hear was silence; the world about him had ceased functioning temporarily as he stared at his prize, broken upon the floor. But reality soon enough came crashing back over him like a rough surf when one's back is turned, causing him to shout, "Just a moment, I'm almost done!" He dressed himself hurriedly while glancing about the room for a hiding place for his prize. Finally settling on the laundry shoot, Joseph sacrificed the materially maligned to save the abstractly abounding; Joseph sacrificed that which had just redefined his entire life in order to save his own integrity.

Realizing that simply opening the door at that moment would arouse even greater suspicion, Joseph flushed the toilet and washed his hands as a rouse. Once finished, he shouted once more at the door, "Back up!" and waited for a response. With the banging and shouting from the other side not yet quelled, Joseph again shouted, "Hey! I said, SHUT THE FUCK UP!" After the briefest of pauses he continued, "Move back and I'll come out."

The door slowly opened, delivering Joseph to the frenzied mob. Questions of location were bellowed by those tearing at his clothing and searching his pockets. Unsatisfied with their lack of results, the throng of boys ransacked the bathroom, again to no avail. Seeing an opening, Joseph furtively shuffled backwards as he watched the destruction unfold. Once he reached the door he ran out of the building and across the lawn, finding solace under a large chestnut tree in an isolated corner of the campus where he remained alone until sundown several hours later.

When he finally withdrew from his trance he arose he caught a glimpse of something spectacular across the pond. Finding himself impelled to get a better look at the fiasco unfolding before his eyes, he immediately began to race around the edge of the pond towards the gathering on its opposite shore. Finding a circle of young boys and girls surrounding another young boy who was lying bloodied on the ground, Joseph acted upon instinct and asked no one in particular, "What is happening here?!"

"He was holding the hand of another boy! He's gay!" came from somewhere in front of him and off to the right; it was far too dark under the moonless sky for Joseph to discern the exact young boy who spoke those words.

"Yeah! So we're kicking his queer ass!" came from another from even further right.

Appalled at what he had just heard, Joseph rushed into the center of the circle, tackling the boy who had just found the 'courage' to take his turn at savagely beating the bloody, suffering pulp. Recognizing that it was Thomas, the ringleader from before, did not dissuade Joseph from throwing a vicious elbow into the face of his classmate. And he did not stop there; Joseph followed the elbow by a series of punches, each thrown wit has much force as he could muster, each landing bluntly on the nose. Too fatigued and aghast at his own actions to continue the annihilation of the animal that lay beneath him, Joseph slowly arose, shouting at the entire crowd, "What is wrong with you people?! Look at what you've done! You *all* did this! You should be ashamed of yourselves!" The crowd, which had dropped into an absolute silence, was too irresolute to mutter even an acknowledging groan of their own role in the massacre. Joseph helped the boy up and began to carry him towards the infirmary. "He could have died!" This contemptible truth, which began somewhere deep within his viscera, giving it an audibly guttural quality, was paired with the most shaming countenance Joseph could muster in an effort to demonstrate to the crowd the despicable nature of their crime.

After reaching the infirmary and ensuring that the victim was going to be okay, Joseph gave some encouraging words to the victim, words which garnered a feeble smile in response, and marched to the cafeteria where he sat quietly among the group of students who had each been at some time ostracized by the cruelty of the more popular schoolboys, for he was certain that this would henceforth be his new clique. It was then that the chef emerged from the kitchen, carrying the silver platter from which he served the seafood stew.

CHAPTER 3

Switching the old platter for the new, the chef served Joseph braised lamb shanks with carrots, garnished with gremolata and a single lemon wedge.

Joseph devoured the dish, savoring every bite. The chef had cooked the lamb exquisitely, even going as far as to remove the lid during the final half hour to ensure that the shanks were perfectly browned, and Joseph appreciated the extra effort. Joseph was not supplied with a knife, but the meat was incredibly tender, falling apart at the lightest touch of the small fork he was provided.

The last time Joseph had had lamb so exquisite was in his youth, amongst friends at a formal dinner with the nearby girls only school. He was sitting at a table with his new friends, the ostracized band of misfits, with not a girl around. The boys sat around talking about their meal as an excuse to avoid the pressing matter of finding a date to the dance on the following evening, an activity around which the entire dinner was designed.

The memories came flooding back. Joseph had still not yet divulged to his new acquaintances in full detail the true nature of the day on which they had so readily absorbed him. They naturally knew of his heroics of that particular evening, everyone at both schools had learned of his gallantry in only a matter of hours, but of his secret only he knew. Many of the other boys at the table had fears of their own, fears ranging from worries of where one may uncover the confidence to ask a girl to be their date to foreknowledge of rejection due to unreserved admissions of one's own assumed physical unattractiveness. But Joseph was both bold and striking. He had neither any issues in conversing with even the prettiest of the girls nor concerns about rejection; he knew that he could win a date if he so chose. His worries, rather, were due to the ambivalence he maintained regarding his own newly made uncertain sexuality.

He was deliberating whether or not to attend the dance; while attendance was mandatory, there were always means to an unseen escape. The issue in his mind was whether or not he truly wanted to escort a girl to the dance. That afternoon in the bathroom not so long ago had left the lasting impression that he, like the boy he rescued, belonged ultimately with another boy. But he also longed for the sense of normalcy and acceptance in life that came with a female companion. He thought he was normal, but the uncertainty nevertheless clung tightly. As the dinner was coming to an end he and his new friends began to take their leave and make the long, depressing walk back to the dormitory, a walk which was really an admission of failure. They had pushed their chairs under the table and nearly made it to the grandiose entryway into the cafeteria when one of the girls, in fact, the girl who had received by far the most attention from the boys that night, had bolted from her chair. She caught Joseph as he stood directly underneath of the open doorframe, gilded in gold, and scolded him.

"Joseph! Where do you think you are going?" Her tone was disapproving, as if he should have known better than to up and leave unannounced.

"We were just leaving," he muttered almost under his breath. The expression caught the young girl off guard because, though it was almost inaudible, it clearly was not the mumbling of a boy too shy to speak to a girl such as her, such as she had become all too accustomed that evening. Rather, his tone was one of an honest and willingly admitted melancholy.

"Well," she finally continued, "you aren't leaving without asking me to the dance tomorrow night."

"And why should I do that?"

"Because I heard about what you did that night for that poor boy and I can't imagine going to this dance with anyone else."

"But wouldn't a more handsome or richer boy make for a better date?"

"No." Joseph finally looked up, meeting her gaze, before she continued. "No they wouldn't. You are an amazing person, Joseph; you are an amazing *man*."

That last word struck a chord with Joseph, reminding him that the definition of a man as one with ethics and genuine intentions and what was known by the boys of his school to be a man were not one in the same. Their definition was flawed; hers was perfect. Accompanying this recognition was another;

Joseph realized that he had just met someone, a woman, who wanted to be with him solely for the person he was.

"Okay." Then, with a smile, "Will you go to the dance with me?"

"No."

Joseph stared back in disbelief. Perhaps he was right in his recent assumption that he did not belong with a girl. But before he could respond with an inquiry into why she had rejected him, she answered his question.

"I'm kidding, of course!" Seeing the relief wash over Joseph's face, she added, "I asked you to ask me, didn't I?" The two smiled back at one another and Joseph returned to his dormitory.

He slept incredibly well that night, feeling certain of himself and his sexuality for the first time since the incident. As he lied in his bed he had an epiphany; the young girl he had met at dinner and was now taking to the dance in less than twenty-four hours was the most beautiful thing he had ever seen. He adored her integrity; the fact that she appreciated him for his ethics, for who he was as a human being, was both refreshing and something he concluded immediately upon observation. But the physical beauty she possessed had for the most part escaped him during their conversation. The more he fixated upon the memory he had of her appearance, her arresting eyes, her tight-lipped serenity which was occasionally punctuated by a smile of plum lips and white teeth, her slender yet somehow unmistakably womanly physique, the more he felt attracted to her sexually.

When he awoke the next morning she still consumed his thoughts, his desires even, desires which were readily and selfishly propagandizing. He had many more hours to go before the dance, and with a lingering fear that he may sway himself away from the enthusiasm he felt for her, Joseph passed the day with his friends. They were exuberant in their praise for their no longer lonely friend, telling Joseph that if he was careful to handle every minor situation that may occur throughout the evening, he might be able to end his night no longer single, perhaps even with his first kiss.

Such thoughts were alluring to Joseph, but he wanted an absolute distraction from her, one which would not permit any reminiscing, so that he might be able to take her hand with the same enthusiasm with which he left her at the dinner the night before.

When the time finally came for the dance, the boys were all aligned against one of the long side walls of the gymnasium where they awaited the entry of the girls. After the girls had finally made their way into the gymnasium and taken their places along the identical wall opposite the boys, Joseph, along with the other boys in attendance, which at this point still included all of Joseph's new friends who were without a date, walked towards the girls to take the hand of their date and escort them to the dance floor.

"Hi Joseph," she giggled as he offered her his arm.

"Hi Mary," he returned with a coy grin.

The two began to dance, twirling about and smiling at each other, though conspicuously silent throughout the evening. Joseph welcomed the silence; it was the perfect opportunity to reflect on each moment passing by, the perfect opportunity to determine whether or not he was truly enjoying himself in the romantic company of a girl. When the festivities ended, long after all of Joseph's new friends had taken their clandestine leaves, one by one, in a meticulously preordained fashion, Mary asked Joseph to escort her back to her dormitory, a unidirectional walk of half an hour.

"Aren't you going to hold my hand?" she asked of him with a passive-aggressively sweet sternness. Joseph answered by blushing and quickly taking a light grasp of her hand, making sure to interlock his fingers with hers. The eroticism of the shared corporeality was so enticing that Joseph now found himself truly hoping for a kiss before their walk was over; Joseph had now found what he felt to be his true sexuality.

They made small talk during their walk, the kind of small talk made by two relative strangers getting to know one another. Topics of discourse ranged from schoolwork to friends, eventually leading to what young couples are supposed to do. The conversation was foreign to Joseph, his naiveté in such matters left him fumbling through trite thoughts and clichéd responses. The final few minutes of their walk felt to Joseph like an eternity, yet another cliché he recognized as it passed through his anxious mind.

But finally the walk ended and they stood facing one another awkwardly, as if something important was supposed to happen, but only if it were initiated by the other. Joseph wondered whether he should try to kiss her or if he was supposed to ask her to be his official girlfriend. Finally, giving in to his lascivious desires without saying a word, Joseph closed his eyes and began to lean towards her. He stretched his neck out and down as he reached his face towards hers. The moment that his lips met hers the relief he felt consumed him, though only momentarily, as his lust immediately took control, permanently burying the doubts he had of his sexuality and filling him with the greatest ecstasy he had ever known.

"So, now that you're my boyfriend, you have to come visit me every weekend and take me to the city."

"Okay." His smile beamed from ear to ear as he watched her walk away, into the dormitory building. Only the day before he had thought that he was gay, and yet here he stood, staring intently at the small but firm derrière working its way up the stairs. While he still felt somewhat ashamed of having had those homosexual thoughts, he nevertheless felt an indescribable joy in learning of his attraction to girls, for being normal meant that his life would not inflict upon him the same tortures that he had witnessed and ended only weeks before in the schoolyard, and after all, he only ever wanted to be happy, to be normal. He felt a deep guilt in associating homosexuality with wrongness, it was never his intention; rather his homosexual thoughts were the completely normal response to the uncertainty of youth. After realizing this while mulling over the happenings of the night, he found a long missing contentment in realizing that he was not gay, that he was young and confused, that he did indeed like girls, that he had had genuine homosexual thoughts and that this was okay, that homosexuality was okay, that he was not homosexual, and, mostly, the overwhelming, nigh indescribable joy of a misfit youth finding conventional normalcy and acceptance in their life.

Now he was normal.

[CHAPTER 4]

The chef served a half salad as a light finish to the meal while the dessert was prepared. After swallowing the final mouthful of lamb and carrot, Joseph turned his attention to the salad. It was the perfect complement to the lamb, containing a sprinkling of coarsely chopped black olives and feta on top of the cucumber, tomato, onion, and arugula mixture which served as the base, and drizzled in balsamic vinegar and olive oil. Though the bites were few, Joseph found himself eagerly anticipating the final dish. He knew not what this would be, but he longed for something sweet and sticky.

Joseph always longed for something more, being reminded of this fact by memories of his fiancée. Mary, having been with Joseph for three years more than a decade, had grown accustomed to his preoccupations. He was always reading something, a necessary obligation for a literary critic and aspiring author, and lately had compounded the distance growing between Mary and he with a piece of criticism of particular interest.

He was determined to make a name for himself as a writer, a determination which led him to the idea of finding a universally successful logical structure which subsumed every literary masterpiece. In so doing he would have both a masterful article which, upon publication, would certainly merit his reputation as a scholar as well as the means by which he could write his own opus magnum, a feat which would cement his place in the annals of history forever. The research project was demanding, consuming nearly every waking moment, leaving to Mary his company only at those extravagant social gatherings which people with their upbringing are required to attend.

But even the parties which he once loved to attend with his beautifully zaftig wife were becoming aggravations, disruptions from his meticulous schedule of investigatory study. The likes of so many great writers, the Plath's, the Solzhenitsyn's, the Khayyam's, the Ibsen's, and lately, the Nabokov's, the Tolkien's, the Kafka's, and the Chopin's, all littered his nightstand, his desk, and of course, his many bookshelves, each work being a physical manifestation of the time he owed to Mary.

"Are you ready to leave yet?"

"Just a moment, let me finish this chapter. I'm nearly finished."

"Joseph! Put that book down this instant! You aren't even dressed yet and we should have left five minutes ago! How I am still engaged to you is the greatest mystery novel of all..."

"Really? *A mystery novel?* How embarrassing. I swear, you are going to be the death of me..."

Half an hour later they were on the road, and with the drive being only fifteen minutes long, they arrived to the party only slightly late.

"Perhaps there is a purpose to all of her nagging," Joseph thought. "I really do take her for granted, thinking of her complaints and criticisms of me with misogynous intent as mere feminine nagging, but it is strictly thanks to her that I am not still hidden away in some corner with a book right now." His thoughts disturbed him, evoking a deep sigh. "If only I were still there, in my study, all alone with my research... I do suppose these things are necessary, especially if I endeavor to make a name for myself."

As the festivities advanced throughout the evening Joseph smiled politely and uttered those ambiguously kind witticisms which are expected in such settings whenever expected and without hesitation. Talk of business and exotic vacations placated the minds of the men with whom Joseph was associating that evening, a positive sign in the mind of Joseph.

Joseph was ordering his third scotch of the night when an old schoolmate by the name of Thomas approached him.

"Joseph! Mary has shared with me the most delightful stories! She talks of you working on some great literary project. I suppose I should have foreseen you becoming an artist, what knowing you and those friends of yours from our old school days."

"Yes, literature indeed! I noticed the two of you talking a while ago, it seems she has taken quite a likening to you Mr. Moore. I just hope you can handle her constant inquiry!" Though he knew that last line of his was despicable, Joseph smiled upon drawing the expected response.

"Oh, Joseph, you know how woman are," he said while rolling his eyes sardonically. "Always bitching about something or other at every last opportunity." He paused momentarily while Joseph smiled in apparent agreement. "But Joseph, that Mary of yours, she's turned into quite the woman. I wouldn't mind being in your shoes, or should I say your bed, if you know what I mean." A jocund elbow and a wink of the eye punctuated his sentence.

"Haha! Yes, Thomas, she is a fine young woman, but you have one of your own if I do say so myself."

Before Thomas could respond, Joseph was pulled aside. "Dear, I see you've met Mr. Moore." Mary flashed a pretty smile in the direction of Thomas before continuing. "But I am really quite tired and ready to go."

"Ah, well, it was truly great speaking to you, Thomas. Perhaps we can all catch up sometime soon over a dinner?"

"That would be fantastic!" said Thomas as Joseph and Mary took their leave.

Ten minutes later and half way home, Mary broke the silence. "You invited Mr. Moore to dinner? You know you're just going to forget and get lost in your books again."

"Mary," he sighed, "that was just friendly banter. None of it meant anything and neither of us expects the other to follow through with the promise."

"But I would really like to see him again, he was charming and so much more pleasant than you are these days. You've really grown quite aloof you know."

"I know, my dear, but I've just been so busy with my work lately. I promise that as soon as I am finished you will have all of my attention; you will be the only subject of my thoughts and the only predicate of my actions. I really do love you." The rest of the ride home continued in silence.

Upon arrival at their house, Joseph proceeded directly to his study and resumed his reading where he had last left it; his research beckoned with the irresistible allure of eagerly anticipated requirement.

"Aren't you coming to bed?"

"Oh give me an hour, won't you?"

"You know, Joseph, you once were, not so very long ago I might add, quite the lover, always there for me; our love was so spontaneous and fey. Now you barely speak except to mutter to yourself while taking notes. It's a wonder you even spoke to anyone at the party." Joseph grunted his acknowledgement, hoping to be left alone to his reading. "You do remember when we first moved into this house, don't you?

"You were so eager to assist, you wanted to make sure everything was so easy and convenient for me. In fact, you even insisted that you carried your library into your new study... Oh in retrospect... Nevertheless, you were so compassionate.

"After we had finally everything settled from the move, you took us to the sea not two days later. The vacation was beautiful, you proposed to me there! On a cliff, overlooking the sea, your words were so deliciously piquant. You promised me everything eternally, a promise in which your every action before, and for the longest time afterwards, was undeniable grounded.

"You even promised me that we would one day soon return there for our honeymoon, but now here you are, more than a year later, hiding in your books, and you haven't even yet begun to solidify our wedding plans. We don't even have a date yet!

"You know, Joseph, you are really making me second guess my decision; you aren't the same magnificently magnanimous man you once were."

"Is that all? I've told you a hundred times, as soon as I am finished with my research you shall have my undivided attention and our wedding day shall swiftly follow." True or not, Joseph had circumnavigated confrontation and further embarrassment.

"Oh my poor Joseph, why can't you be more like that Thomas from the party last night?" Uttering this request, she took her leave and went to bed.

"She is going to be the death of me…"

CHAPTER 5

Again the guard signaled and again the chef emerged with a new platter. This final platter, once uncovered, revealed a dish which Joseph had not had in over a decade. The chef served Joseph baklava.

The man who had earlier sat in the chair behind the desk at the end of the corridor entered the cafeteria just in time to witness the consequences of his earlier quandary. While sitting alone behind his desk after Estel had been escorted, he had decided to violate the laws of the community and serve Joseph baklava. He knew the Estel only ever wanted to protect Joseph, but he also knew that Estel was an incredibly calculated man who would ultimately count upon the trust of an executive to ensure the protection of Joseph when it mattered most. Besides, there was no official record of the earlier conversation, hence he had decided to serve the baklava.

As Joseph spooned the first piece of baklava into his mouth visions of the young woman from earlier waking dream began to race through his mind. Who was she? He certainly knew her once, so where did they first meet? Were they close? These questions burned his psyche, leaving only an insatiable desire to discover the true identity of this mysterious yet captivating ingénue.

"You know this, Joseph! You're so close!" The voice in his head seemed to Joseph to be some sort of third party, omniscient, inner monologue.

"Where is Estel? Why is he not here too?"

"Don't worry about him, he's gone now, powerless. Besides, he doesn't want you to know."

The man from behind the desk at the end of the corridor smiled at this proclamation, leaning into a more comfortable position against the wall where he planned to watch the culmination of the recent developments in the cafeteria, developments which he had invoked.

The vision of the woman was becoming clearer, revealing a continuously looping transformation from child to death. He focused harder on the series of images replaying through his mind. The last of which was a casket with the woman inside, her face still containing so many traces of beauty and youth. Then came the young girl again.

The images progressed, showing the girl growing up before his eyes into a beautiful young woman. "Yes, that is most definitely Mary! But why is she dead? What happened to my Mary?!" His voice echoed angrily across the vacuous dining chamber. But before anyone could respond, not that anyone had the intention to do so, Joseph recalled a hidden memory, one which he had not once processed since it was first formed.

"Joseph, we need to talk." She had entered his study.

"Just a moment dear, let me finish this paragraph please."

"No, Joseph," she said while approaching him from behind. Upon reaching his seated position in front of his desk, Mary gently massaged his shoulders for several moments before divulging the true nature of the conversation she wished to have. "I cannot do this anymore, Joseph. I am leaving you."

The solemnity with which she spoke made the hair on the back of his neck stand upright and his face and arms go numb. Even though he eyes were still directed at the book before him, his pupils had contracted so finely that he could only see a single word, all else was a blur. "Wh-... Why would you do that?" he stammered.

Pulling in a deep breath via her barely open mouth with teeth still clenched and slowly letting it out through her nose, she prepared herself for the vexing admission. She had considered telling him for some months now, ever since the days following the last party they had attended together, but with the recent development of the past week, she had meant to tell him each and every of the past six days. For some reason today was the day on which she found the courage to initiate the intimidating intercourse about her immature incipience.

"Joseph, I am pregnant."

The words were hallowing, but Joseph summoned the words to a response, however creaky and wavering these words may have been. "How can you leave me just as our child is to be born? We are supposed to be getting married."

"Yes, that is just the thing. We are supposed to already be married, my love. And yet we are not. That is why... That is why my transgression occurred."

"Transgression? What transgression?"

"Joseph... Oh how do I say this... The baby inside of me, well..." She hesitated for a moment before she blurted out the truth. "It's not yours!"

Seeing that Joseph had nothing to say, Mary began to cry relentlessly. "It's Thomas! He's the father!" she screamed at him through sobs. "At least he spends time with me!" She ran towards the door where she turned only to say, "I'm going to stay with him from now on, keep your precious books! Goodbye!" She was gone.

"The only woman I have ever loved is out of my life forever!" With Mary now gone, impregnated by another man, he entered a hysteria of angry shouting and intense bouts of crying until the muscles in his sides thoroughly ached. To Joseph there was only one thing a man in his position could do; pouring himself a tall glass of scotch he began to finish his exquisitely deft literary article on the universality of certain concepts in the greatest masterpieces of the literary arts.

Seeing its completion in under an hour, Joseph fetched his pistol. Pouring himself one last drink, which he downed in one long swallow, he loaded a single bullet and placed the pistol in his mouth. "I always knew she would be the death of me... I must not live my life if I must live it without my love." The words were muffled, unintelligible to anyone who may have been interested in listening at that moment, not that anyone was around. Joseph was alone in the world, both physically and metaphorically at that moment.

But he could not shake his love for Mary so easily. While killing himself would end his pain, the pain she had caused him, it would only antagonize her forever. This pain, he decided, was far worse than death, and, though she may very well deserve such a fate, he loved her too much to bestow upon her such ceaseless torture. And yet someone must die; of this he was certain.

He tucked the pistol into his waist and drove towards Thomas's house. The two expecting lovers raced into the front yard upon Joseph's arrival, offering half-hearted though sincerely phrased apologies while sternly asking him to leave. But Joseph would have none of this; the words passed by him without comprehension; his sole focus was on the task at hand. He removed the pistol from his waist and pointed it at Mary.

"Joseph, NO!" Mary begged in a high-pitched, shrieked plea.

"Joseph, stop it! Point the gun at me, *kill me!*" Thomas, remembering the beating he had received from the hands of Joseph that night by the pond in grade school, was not underestimating the seriousness of Joseph's intentions.

"Okay." His voice was unnervingly quiet.

"Run, Mary!"

Without reservation, Joseph leveled his aim at Thomas's face. "Turn to the side, to your right. Stop right there." Thomas now stood before Joseph in a position which offered the shooter a perfect vantage of his left temple. "Won't be the first time I've hit you there, now will it be?"

"Joseph!" Thomas was now begging. "Please don't do this! Think of the baby!"

Without flinching Joseph pulled the trigger, once. Watching Thomas fall dead, limp on the ground before him, Joseph directed his attention towards Mary. She had not fled during the murder of her new lover; she had been far too fixated upon the horror before her to even contemplate her escape. Seeing Joseph turn towards her, however, awakened her instincts and she took off at a full sprint into the house. She tried to lock the door behind her, but he crashed his way into the house with overwhelming brute force. She raced down the long, narrow hallway which emitted itself from the open entry foyer. His shot was completely unobstructed; he raised his gun and pulled the trigger. Nothing happened. Due to his original intentions he had only loaded a single bullet. Throwing the gun down in disgust, Joseph ran towards her at a demanding clip, short enough of an all-out sprint to ensure that he remained agile and in control.

She had fled into the kitchen and hidden behind the island, armed with a small steak knife. Even though Joseph had not seen her grab the knife, he could hear her breathing, thus he knew where she was. Grabbing a knife en route to the far side of the island, he noticed that only one other knife was missing from the block. Assuming she had it on her person, Joseph began to walk wide around the right side of the island, hesitating for a moment to grab an overhanging frying pan as he reached level with the front side of the island. He toyed with the idea of using it defensively, but a far better idea struck him. He threw it down over the island, just left of where he knew Mary to be.

As soon as it hit the floor he thrust the knife forward. Having bolted away from the frying pan in fear, she turned the corner at full speed, running belly first onto the largest blade in the kitchen of her late new lover.

Her wrist went limp and the steak knife fell to the floor. Kicking it away, Joseph cleared a place on the floor where he intended to slowly lower his fiancée. Her eyes were as wide as her agape mouth and her hands clutched her wound, but she could not muster even a whimper. "Why did you do this to me?"

"I didn't mean to, Joseph, I swear. I just wanted to feel loved is all."

"You know I'm going to kill you." There was no mistaking this gruffly uttered statement as a question.

"Yes, I know. Just make it quick." Joseph did not respond other than by raising the knife to her throat. "I love you Joseph."

"I love you too." The knife dashed across her throat.

He waited a minute, ensuring that she was dead before he continued. His sole thought was in digging out the baby which had destroyed his life. He slashed back and forth with the knife, scooping pieces of her viscera with the side of the knife blade and flinging it aside where it stuck to the cabinetry, slowly dripping down to the floor. He knew he would not find a fetus, Mary was showing no signs of her pregnancy, and he had no idea which of the many slaughtered organs was the womb, so he lifted her skirt entirely above the now gaping wound and prepared to gouge what remained of her lower abdomen. But something was wrong. He had glimpsed it in passing as he slit her panties with the knife but had not registered it during that brief observation. It took nearly thirty second of looking about his vicinity to find it again, but there it was, dangling on the floor, a thin white string in between her legs; she was menstruating. The tale of the bastard baby of Mary was a lie.

She had not left him because she was pregnant; no, that was only a lie concocted to validate her decision. She had left him because she no longer loved him and she longed to be with Thomas. But he had killed them both. He flung the knife across the room where it smacked into the window, off of which it bounced before coming to a rest on the tile floor.

Moments later, or rather six hours by the clock, Joseph finally arose from his position crouched over her now cold corpse. "How had so much time passed?" he thought as he bolted through the front door of the house of his former classmate now twice assaulted by his hands.

"Don't worry about that Joseph, just get home." It was Estel. His advice was both commonsensical and urgent. Joseph, with an unequivocal obedience, obliged his counterpart and returned home swiftly.

Thomas's house was isolated, just past the outskirts of town and by the river, so nobody would find the bodies anytime soon. Now composed thanks to Estel, Joseph walked calmly into his study and began reading, as if the events of that day had been at most insipid. He read, and read, and read, and read some more. Three sleepless days passed before there came a knock on his door.

With no answer from within, the armed men barged their way into the house and continued to call for Joseph, continuously to no avail. Finally, as they approached the study and called for Joseph yet again, a reply came.

"Joseph is not here right now!" The voice was an eerily capricious falsetto.

"Who is that, and are you in the study?"

"My name is Edna, and yes I am. I'm reading Lewis and eating baklava!" The exclamation was gleefully fey and girlish in tone.

The armed men approached with caution to find a foul smelling grown man who was clearly in need of a shave and wearing a blood encrusted suit reading *The Screwtape Letters*. The sight was terrifying, but the armed men crept closer to their target.

"What can I do for you?"

"Are you or are you not Joseph?"

"No, I told you, I'm Edna."

"Do you have any identification on you, Edna? Or a wallet?"

"Maybe! I don't know!"

"Can you check you jacket pockets, please?

"Oh! Look! Here's one!" Edna handed the wallet over to her interrogator.

"I see… Well, Edna is it? Do you think you can come with us to the station?"

"Can I bring my book with me?" The armed men drew yet more fear and anxiety from this perplexity, but handcuffed their intended target and left for the police station nonetheless. The book remained behind.

At the police station the officers locked their arrest into an interrogation room, all alone. After an hour an officer walked into the room and gave the criminal a cheese sandwich and a small black coffee. Citing more paperwork to process before they could interrogate him, the officer left the room without answering any questions. "Can I have my book?" But it was too late, the door had closed behind the officer.

Four hours later three different officers entered the room, one with a clipboard and an envelope, each with a cup of coffee. "How long is this going to take?"

"How long is what going to take?"

"Look, just confess. We know you did it. You're covered in their blood. It was your fiancée in his house and now they both are dead. What happened? Was she messing around behind your back?"

"I'm hungry and tired and I want my book!" The words came in a high pitched, exhausted defiance.

"You can have your book if you confess to the murders."

"But I didn't kill anybody! All I do is read! Read, read, read, read, read!"

"But-"

"Annnnnnnd READ!" Edna was now clapping with a joyful fervor.

"Stop it with this voice acting! Right now! Or I'll make you wait another twelve hours, cuffed to this chair without food or water. You'll be my dog! No, you'll be less than a dog! You *are* less than a dog!" The officer reached across the table, slapped Edna across the face, cuffed her arm to the back of the chair, and left the room with his two colleagues in tow.

Joseph awoke chained to a chair in the middle of a strange room. Footsteps could be heard echoing down a nearby hallway, approaching at an alarming rate. "Joseph! Go back to sleep!"

"Why? And who are you?"

"I got you out of danger before."

"What danger? I don't know you!"

"Ah. You are worse than I thought. Look, just trust me, you don't want to be here when they walk through that door."

The door to the interrogation room opened and the three men from before returned. "Let me guess, you must be Edna?" His sarcasm was palpable.

"No. I am Estel."

"Fuck me. Fine! Estel. Did Joseph kill Mary and Thomas?"

"Why don't you ask Joseph?" The words were as unruffled as they were gruff.

"Why don't you stop fucking around before I beat the shit out of you for real this time? Would you like that?"

Again calmly, "Why do you want a confession? Do you not have sufficient evidence?"

"We have enough evidence to have you executed. Twice." Pausing for a moment to make eye contact with each of his two counterparts, the officer continued. "Everything we are doing is for your sake."

"You mean for Joseph's sake?"

Three simultaneous nods began the choreography. The primary officer slowly walked his way around the table to Estel along with one of his two colleagues while the third, the nearest to the lone window in the room, repositioned his body along the back wall so that it obstructed any view in or out of the window. Estel held his head high as he was surrounded, but this did not last long. He had his arms ripped behind his back and held in place by one of the officers while the primary officer punched him in the gut.

"Why did you kill them?" Another vicious blow to the gut prevented any answer to the yelled inquiry. "I said, why did you *kill* them?!" On the word 'kill' another blow, this time to the face, evincing a bloody gash across the forehead, was delivered.

"ANSWER ME!" The words echoed throughout the entire police station and were followed by a frenzy that left Estel bloodied and bruised from head to waist. After the fifty second tumult ceased, the primary officer took a deep breath, ran his hand through his hair, and collected himself.

"Did Joseph kill Mary and Thomas? Because if he did, he might be eligible for those newfangled lethal injection drugs. But if he claims he didn't or doesn't answer me right now, he will get the electric chair, the electric chair with a dry sponge if I'm any good at what I do."

Estel felt his eyes dilate, no person deserved such a terrible fate. "If Joseph did it, you can assure that it's not the chair?"

"That depends, did Joseph kill those people?"

With no other alternative available, Estel caved, for Joseph. "Yes."

"See? Was that so bad? And since I'm a good, honest man, a man of my word, a man you can trust, Joseph can get those needles. Take him to holding, boys!" The man holding Estel by the arms lifted Estel up and out of the chair, and the man covering the window helped carry Estel away to the prison cell which would hold him until the trial.

Weeks later, weeks of uninterrupted solitude save for two meals a day, a judge met with Estel inside of the prison cell. "Joseph?" called the judge as he entered the cell.

"Estel."

"Ah, I see. Well, I am the judge that presided over Joseph's case. As I am sure you aware, Joseph is not in any condition to enter a public courtroom. Given the graphic nature of his crime, the way he murdered that poor Mary, slaughtered really, we took his confession as a guilty plea. Because of the guilty plea Joseph will be spared the electric chair, instead being put to death ten years, a month, and six days from today via lethal injection. That and we will be recommending a psychiatrist monitor Joseph and have daily counsel with the condemned."

"I think it would be better if I attended those meetings in his stead."

"Perhaps that will be the case anyways," muttered the judge as he took his leave. Pausing in the doorway just as he was about to be rid of Estel forever, the judge turned to say, "If you happen to see Joseph, do let him know for me?" The question was rhetorical, ending with a sharp turn and the slamming of the jail cell door as its perfect punctuation.

[CHAPTER 6]

"Joseph, how was the baklava?" asked the man whose desk was against the brick wall at the end of the long corridor.

"Oh my god," he whispered to himself. "I killed her..."

With a hedonistic grin upon his face, "Tell me, Joseph, how much have you remembered?"

"Everything." The word was so harrowingly spoken that the man from behind the desk felt a darkly disturbing chill. "But tell me, what of my prison stay? I can't remember any of that. I can remember my life from adolescence to her death, I can recall the actions of my friends afterwards, from seeing Mary post-mortem through my imprisonment, but I can't place myself directly in any of the scenes that I can remember from after the murder... How long have I been here?"

"You've been here for a day less than a decade a month and a week now, Joseph. You really can't remember anything from these past ten years?"

"No! I cannot!"

"Nothing before today?"

"No!"

"Well, what did you learn today?"

"Edna and Humbert and Estel are apparently my roommates."

"Roommates?"

"Yes, they are my roommates. I feel like I've known them for years and years, but I can't recall anything of them, aside from Estel. He was always there to protect me."

"Protect you from what?"

"From you."

"From me? Why from me?"

"Because… I suppose because he never wanted me to remember what…happened."

"You mean what you did."

"Yes, what I did." Joseph let out a deep sigh after his first admission of guilt.

"Why would he do that?"

"I don't know. I don't even know who he is! I never even met him until I killed Mary."

"And how exactly did you two meet?"

"I'm not entirely certain. He was just kind of there to protect me and ensure I got home safely after the…incident. I can't even remember anything from after then until today."

"What does he look like?"

"What do you mean? You've seen him. He looks like…" Joseph's voice trailed off as he realized that he could not quite place a single detail of his roommate.

"You don't know what he looks like? You've seen him."

"Yes, but…"

"But what?"

"But I don't think I've actually ever seen him in person. At the, um, scene, you know, of the accident, and even here in the community, he always just talks to me, I never actually see him."

"Interesting. And what about Edna and Humbert?"

Joseph's breathing became shallow and fast and his eyes went wide as he realized, "I haven't seen them either, only heard from them."

"Let's focus on Estel for a moment again, shall we? Why would someone else take so much care of you, live with you, go to such lengths to ensure your safety, particularly someone you don't even know? Who would even do such a thing? Who would be so interested in your wellbeing?"

"I don't know! I was never even that close to anybody besides Mary, and she is dead! There isn't another person in the entire world who would care that much about my wellbeing!"

Pausing for a moment to regain an emotional homeostasis and a calm control of the room, the man from behind the desk asked Joseph, "So then who is Estel?"

"The fuck if I know! Look at me now! I'm angry and shouting; I'm nothing like myself anymore! This is why I would never let you talk to me!"

The man from behind the desk took a step back and raised his eyebrows, relieved that the worst was now safely over. "*You* never let me talk to you?" His eyebrows were still raised, giving them the appearance of permanent features frozen onto his countenance.

"No I don't!... Wait, *I'm* the one who hasn't been letting me talk to you… *I am Estel!*"

"Yes! Finally! After ten years, we've finally done it Joseph!" The man from behind the desk leapt into the air with a big, toothy grin in utter jubilation.

"But, wait, what? I'm so confused…What is going on here?"

"Shall I tell you of the past ten years? Of the imprisonment which you cannot remember? Of the details of our sessions?"

"Sessions?"

"Yes, sessions. See Joseph, I have been meeting with you ever since you arrived here. I have been talking with you for the past ten years, well, with Estel, and at first with Edna, but with you for the past ten years nevertheless.

"When you first came here Estel had served his purpose so Edna became your only persona for over a year. You expressed yourself, your true self from what I gather, with some of the other inmates, but apparently it wasn't quite right because Edna grew frustrated and Estel returned. Humbert, too, as a matter of fact, though he was a rarity throughout your entire stay. Edna would come out to play on many occasions, but once Estel reappeared, all of my progress, all of *our* progress, was stalled by his constant thwarting. He was there strictly to protect you, and he almost succeeded in preventing me from ever getting to you, the real you that is."

"Wait, so, I'm insane? Schizophrenic or something?"

"How much exactly do you want to know?"

"Just… I was insane for a while, no?"

"Yes."

"And now, at least for the moment, I am sane again for the first time in over a decade, right?"

"Exactly."

"Then that is all."

"You are certain?"

"Yes, I am certain. This is so overwhelming, and I won't be able to process anything more. This is enough for my mind for now."

"Fair enough, Joseph. That means it is time for you to meet with the priest."

"Finally..." The muttered words again struck a chord with the psychiatrist.

"What do you mean finally? Did you know about your meeting with the priest today?"

"Yes, I did. That is the whole reason I got out of bed today."

"Now that is encouraging..." A sardonic grin emerged below the long, crooked nose of the man from behind the desk at the end of the corridor. "Well, if you are sure that there are no more questions, then it is time to have your meeting. Follow me."

"Shouldn't he be chained?" The two guards from before were still in the cafeteria, and the first was only wanting to perform his duties with the utmost responsibility.

"No, it is okay. If he doesn't want to be chained, let him be free for a moment. You don't want to be chained again, do you Joseph?"

"No, I would really rather not. You have my word, I will behave."

"Okay, follow me."

The four men walked out of the cafeteria and across the prison to the medical ward. The room was busy with a doctor and a small series of nurses running to and fro, finalizing their preparations for the execution, and yet there was the priest, also awaiting Joseph in the execution room, calmly seated in a chair which sat immediately before the cold, steel table where Joseph would soon die.

"Ah, Joseph. Good to see you. I am the prison appointed priest. Are you ready to meet God, my child?" The priest was an old man with a weathered face, worn from decades of experience in spiritually guiding the executed through their final moments of life. The elaborate robes he wore only exacerbated the pompousness of his appearance, leading Joseph to think of the priest as a wizard rather than a man of the cloth.

"Yes sir, I suppose I am."

"Well then, shall we pray? Cross yourself and bow your head my son." Joseph stared back at the priest, unmoving, but the priest only stared back, clearly waiting for Joseph to obey his command before continuing. Tacitly admitting defeat after several long moments, Joseph made the appropriate religious gesticulations and bowed his head in obedience of the ritual.

"Dear Father, who art in Heaven, please welcome this, man, into your Kingdom. He may have strayed far from you intended path during his life, but here now, in his final moments, he is accepting Jesus into his life as his Lord and

Savior. He is genuinely sincere in apology and he humbly asks for your forgiveness.

"We now heed Your word in the final hours of this man's life. To quote from Your word, Isaiah 40:28 says: 'Do you not know? Have you not heard? The Everlasting God, the LORD, the Creator of the ends of the earth does not become weary or tired. His understanding is inscrutable.' Thus, Lord, we know that You will understand the true actions of this man more clearly than any of us men ever could; You will be his ultimate Judge. For You never tire, You never fatigue, and thusly You have seen all that this man has done so that You may deliver upon him his eternal fate with Absolute wisdom.

"But again we heed Your Word. Leviticus 24:17 says: 'And he that kills any man shall surely be put to death.' This man is only obeying your Law, fulfilling his punishment as You have prescribed. And after all, Your Prescriptions are the basis for a Good and Just ethics. By paying his dues, perhaps then You can truly forgive him, absolving him of all of his sins, not only the brutal murder of his wife and the man who stole her."

Joseph felt out of place and highly uncomfortable with the ongoing communication on his behalf, showing it with consternation on his face, though the priest continued aware.

"This is the beauty of Your Prescriptions. To denote the Ultimate Law as You have done is an act of irreproducible brilliance, for no man can be moral, nor can any civilization can be just, without an Ultimate Basis from which all actions originate. Man, and civilization created in its image, is an intrinsically flawed object, rightfully undeserving of Your Love.

No matter how hard we try, we, man, shall never truly begin to mimic what you have created unless we directly adhere to Your Laws. And yet Your Writing guides us towards Your Love and, as the most benevolent reward of all, our Eternal Salvation. But I digress on the infinite distance between the jurisprudence of man and that of the Divine.

"I remind You now, Father, that we, men, have adhered to Your Prescriptions, not for our sake, but for that of the soon departed. However, for the sake of this man, albeit the case that he is a murderer, I must remind you of yet another of Your Laws. Leviticus 20:10: 'If there is a man who commits adultery with another man's wife, one who commits adultery with his friend's wife, the adulterer and the adulteress shall surely be put to death.' Perhaps then, my Lord, this man, this Joseph, was merely fulfilling Your Bidding, for, though his actions appear unjust, his actions did indeed exact the proper punishment as Your Law prescribes. Your Commands should not be questioned, for as is said in the Good Book, 1 Kings 20:35-36: 'Meanwhile, the LORD instructed one of the group of prophets to say to another man, "Strike me!" But the man refused to strike the prophet. Then the prophet told him, "Because you have not obeyed the voice of the LORD, a lion will kill you as soon as you leave me." And sure enough, when he had gone, a lion attacked him and killed him.' Sometimes the Will of the Lord is confusing, but it comes from an Infinite Wisdom and should not be questioned.

"Now then, with that said, I should take the time to ask for Your forgiveness on the behalf of the two deceased at the hands of Joseph. They were undoubtedly sinners. By Mary committing adultery she most certainly deserved her death; her actions were reprehensible and unmerited, even if her Joseph neglected her in favor of his studies. No matter how neglected a woman is, she belongs with her husband, or in this case her fiancée. A commitment is a commitment, and commitments must inevitably come with some tribulations. So please, Father, please forgive Mary of her misgivings and the man with whom she became an adulteress."

Joseph was deeply confused at the direction of the conversation. He was a murder. He never followed the church. And yet the priest was making him out to be a good Christian, though certainly in the condescending manner befitting a murder.

"Your Word is infallible, the only True Path in life. Without God no man can live a just and moral life; without utter devotion misgivings will inevitably occur, damnable misgivings which condemn a man to the fiery depths of Hell for all eternity. Joseph once thought he was above Your Law, he once thought he could live a life without You. He has seen from his past actions, as have we all, that without You, only evil can emerge. Proverbs 3:7 says: 'Do not be wise in your own eyes; fear the LORD and shun evil.' Fear of the Lord is an unequivocal requirement for a righteous, pious life. By fearing God one hates evil, and to not fear God is to embrace evil. Furthermore, evil nevertheless abounds in the world today, emanating from all of those non-pious men who do not fear God. While this evil should be feared for the harm, the temptations, and the attempts to make one stray from the Path of the Lord that it may bring, always remember that the Lord will always protect the pious man. Those who fear things other than the Lord, fearing these things rather than fearing the Lord, these people are evil, for they fear for their own wellbeing rather than for the wellbeing of the desires of the Lord. They are the ones delivering unto God's great Creation all of the evil we witness, the evil that destroys societies and condemns those of a weaker faith in the Lord to Hell for all eternity. Fear is evil, for fearing things is to fear the Will of the Lord. God controls all, controls everything; it is God that put the Good into the world. To fear is to dislike what the Lord has created, and to dislike the work of the Lord is to be evil. 1 John 4:18 says: 'There is no fear in love; but perfect love casts out fear, because fear invokes punishment, and the one who fears is not perfected in love.' And don't forget Deuteronomy 11:1: 'You shall therefore love the LORD your God, and always keep His charge, His statutes, His ordinances, and His commandments.' Thus one must never fear, for fear brings evil. Love is the proper path, but Joseph let his love wane. This was truly Joseph's greatest crime.

"Now, before I ask one final time for Your Forgiveness on behalf of the condemned, I would like to thank You for all that You have done for us here on earth. As it says in Exodus 31:17: 'It is a sign between me and the sons of Israel forever; for in six days the LORD made Heaven and earth, but on the seventh day He ceased from labor, and was refreshed.' We, Your humble servants, are eternally grateful for Your monumental creation, and thank You and praise You for giving to us a world which took so much from You to create. You are truly a loving God, a God who loves all of Your children.

Please remember this love when Joseph comes unto You here shortly, and remember those who truly love You forever. Amen."

CHAPTER 7

"Okay, Joseph, sit up here on the table." The priest helped Joseph onto the table where his life was to be taken from him in the next few minutes.

"Is everybody ready?" The prison warden looked around the room, noting the nods of approval all around. "Yes? Good. Commence with the execution."

"Lie back on the table Joseph. It is time." The instructions from the doctor were cold and crass.

"Yes sir," Joseph mumbled. His lips were now visibly shaking and a massive dread had overcome his defenses. Things had moved so suddenly. There was no time to savor his dinner. There was only confusion and death. But soon, he knew, the confusion would cease and there would be only death.

"This will all be over soon, just close your eyes and relax." While speaking these words the doctor finished the task of strapping Joseph to the table. Then, reaching for the needle on the nearest counter, the doctor began to count down the final seconds of consciousness Joseph had left to live.

"Five, four, three..."

"Two... one... oh god! oooh! that hurt! ahhh! it feels...hard? my arm is so heavy! I feel... tired... but my oh shit! this is it! this is death! so bright! more oxygen fight off delay breath faster jackass! wait, what? I CAN'T! oh god! my arm! leg! they don't move! why can't I move my arms?! oh my god but talking! they're talking! I can hear them! nooooo! they're gonna inject me with the poison! cold! my leg? fuck! table? I feel it, but how can I feel? why am I not dead? at least I'm why are they leaving? are they gonna let me live? let me live! empty? where did they go? maybe this will all wear off Escape! I can get out make amends live a good life so many beams of light reminds me of dentist office I wish I could move my legs! what is where is the person people I wanna go! if I get out of here I will be so much better I will work with the priest and guy and fix my problems and get back to normal I wonder when they are coming back or is this the end? are these drugs the ones that kill me? did they work? how long do they take or are they going to come back to kill me? fuck them that stupid priest spouting off his dogma he was such hypocrite when but if I fix my life I can become a productive citizen again just focus on my studies oh I would kill to be with my books again! no! I cannot think like that! but it was just an expression but it still can't think like that it's not healthy I must be healthy but these thoughts are bad and I must overcome them and if I do and somehow I live I can atone for everything oh don't let me die! please God! please! I now know the error of my ways! that priest was right your prescriptions I must accept Jesus prescriptions to live my life by so I can atone for everything live and fix everything oh God! I don't want to go to Hell! is this Hell? maybe I died and I am already in Hell and this this would be the worst fate imaginable uncertain if my death is imminent or merely lurking behind the next moment and lying here and I can't control anything and I can barely breathe why can I breathe if I have no control over any of my other muscles? this is a fate no one should suffer but why am I suffering? do I deserve this? is this fair? what is fair? when does a person deserve to die? wasn't this her fault anyways? that God damn Mary wait I mean I'm sorry God I didn't mean that I shouldn't call upon you like that and besides she I'm sure doesn't deserve such a fate besides wasn't her action only a consequence of my actions? did I kill her before I ever killed her? did I kill myself? does that count as suicide? if that is suicide then does that mean that I cannot get into Heaven even if I repent here my final moments and truly accept Jesus and genuinely ask for forgiveness? fuck god! god is horrible god is the devil who would write such laws? god should go to hell he needs to leave his stupid heaven and go to hell go here come here and suffer as I suffer for he knows not what he inflicts upon his children haha! listen to me I am speaking like I am god I *am* God! I am Jesus! I killed Mary! but god and Mary had a baby but Jesus was that baby but Jesus and god are the same person that is stupid fuck Jesus! Jesus abandoned me here all alone and put me flawed and broken in an even worse world that and I yes it was the world's fault that I did what I did not mine nothing ever was my fault it was all causal and uncontrollable but then this is uncontrollable and my fate is inevitable and I AM GOING TO DIE! NOOOO! I DON'T WANT TO DIE! I DON'T DESERVE THIS! PLEASE GOD! PLEASE! I BEG OF YOU! oh my god this is no use I know better than this but I don't want to die and I am scared why is this happening to me I don't don't I don't I don't deserve this PLEASE! why can't I actually speak? why would anyone willingly and knowingly murder someone who is awake? mentally ill? isn't this genocide? didn't we as humans just kill Hitler to prevent the same thing from happening the killing of people believed to be subhuman when really I just need help why couldn't I be a Jew? why can't I just be me? alive and not here somewhere else but who am I? that doctor kept talking to me always about them about me that was me I know that was me but why what was the problem with me there had to be a problem if he kept after me like that what could it be? everybody here is a fucking murder or something else bad and never get this kind of attention so why me? I wonder why me maybe there was something else but what could it be? I remember so little of these past how long have I been here oh fuck I don't even know when it is except it's time to die now oh fuck why are they killing me? they're killing me because I killed Mary but why did I do that because she was a fucking whore bitch cheating whore bitch fuck FUCK! even she didn't deserve it but she lied to me she wasn't even fucking pregnant she wasn't even honest with me she could ask just ask me to leave I'd hate her but she could have left but she lied to me alive still but no that was her mistake too still not fitting but why do they want to kill me now? shit on them it must be something else but the only other thing I can remember is all of these memories that came to me over lunch today about killing her and my childhood? that's weird some guilty memories about uncertainty over who I was because I didn't ever belong but does that warrant killing me? no way I got lucky and found somebody and was normal not that normal matters because come on I mean if can tell you that something is okay even though it caused me turmoil once and wasn't even me who I am why are they killing me for that? oh what the fuck I'm delusion they kill me now because I killed her I killed Mary so I get to be killed maybe that is fair but why like this?! I can fix who I am and just be good and ethical and work even fuck I'll be a slave forever just let me live then I wouldn't need any help then I would be a perfectly fine human being but now I am dead and nobody will help me I just said then a lot then then then then wow I am actually kinda bored right now am I coming to terms with my own fate? funny how imminent death brought on one of the longest uninterrupted thoughts of my life I wonder how many times I have ever thought that long without distractions like these walls are so annoying all white with tiny little imperfections chips in the paint the walls in Germany aren't this bad are they I wonder but all I've ever known is my city and the sea I wish I were on vacation what if this was a vacation and I was asleep and I was dreaming and I'm about to wake up and go play in the sand and swim in the surf what if I were eaten by a shark? wouldn't that be fitting if I were dreaming and I woke up and my from my nightmare and I was shark eaten by a shark it would be so ironic I do love irony if only the irony of my death could be known if they could know how I suffer those other people and save me PLEASE SAVE ME! I don't want to die! oh my god I just wasted the last minute I guess a minute or two or three or less I don't know talking about but I'm not talking I'm only thinking thinking inside my head all alone and about to die what was I thinking about? I can't remember and I'm sitting here thinking well technically lying here strapped to a table which really seams unnecessary since I can't even move my muscles I wonder if they think I'm dead yet WHAT WAS I THINKING ABOUT?! there was something and I can't recall it and I'm just wasting my time oh yes! that was it! I am about to die and I'm just wasting my last moments of cognizance with stupid ramblings and I could at least I'm still thinking you know this could be so much worse…

"wow I guess I just blanked out for a second I hope it was only a second and I'm wasting my last moments of life of self-awareness rambling about wasting my time my last time alive and I'm going to die what is death like? will this hurt or will I just suddenly not be aware of the world? the world won't even be aware of me after I die only occasionally the other prisoners and guards and wardens and the doctor they might think about me and they might share my story but probably not and then they will die and there will be no memory of me and to think I spent so much time working on my grandiloquent plot to my masterpiece and I will never get to tell it what a shame but what if I wasn't going to be any good as a writer but how else I wanted to be such a great writer the best ever or at least unforgettable no the best really the best the best ever but I can't do that now I wonder what it's like when you are dead and you leave a lasting impression on the world and other people think about you and remember and study your work but that won't ever happen there won't be any little boys or girls in China or Alaska studying my work ever because I never got the chance to write it this isn't fair! none of this is fair! I don't want to die! please don't let me die! I'm thirsty wouldn't a beer be fantastic right now it so would like that time when I was at the place with the cabinets in here are so haunting probably because I know what they hide the poison which is in my veins and is going to kill me turn me into nothing forevermore leaving me a nameless unknown abstraction forgotten by all of existence what could be a worse fate than that? I would rather suffer as I am now than suffer as I shall for eternity perhaps that is Hell? being forgotten eternally as I shall be like when I went to the prison the whole world forgot about me has the whole world outside of this prison forgotten me already? I forgot myself so it only figures and numbers and equations oh if this is the torment literature brought me perhaps I should have studied math rather than trying to become an artist u v w x y z it's like I can see letters in my head but I'm doing it again! I have to stop letting my brain stop working it takes it too long to restart it's like one of those giant computer things like they had at the university where it takes so much time to restart whenever they stop working on their research and stuff and I wish my brain was like a computer but what if it is? what if it is just a computer that feels emotion and is more complicated than any computer we have ever built? what if one day people build computers that are more compassionate than humans? but if my brain is just a computer that makes sense because everything is causal anyways and if everything if causal then maybe it really wasn't my fault so if everything is causal and people are so smart and we think we know so much about the world all around the globe everywhere around the world across the seas and oceans I'm doing it again then if we think we know so much about everything and existence itself then If everything is causally defined then why do we kill people for things like murder? isn't it actually everyone's fault when any one person gets killed from murder? because if any one of us had done any one thing different then that one person would never have been murdered and how is it fair that that one individual murderer is killed when their action is the culmination of a series of events preceding it which was irreversible and unavoidable so isn't it everyone's fault? but then what right do I have to live? even if I had no control over my actions then what right does anyone have to live? we're all just computers input output nothing more that's it nobody deserves to live we just live we should just sanctify life and worship and forget free will no free will there is no free will we just do based on the past and the moment and the what we think of it future the future we don't know the future that's as good as free will that's what gives life meaning uncertainty we don't know I don't know do we know? we no no we don't know it and fuck it what even is morality? it sure as hell isn't all that priest Jesus shit we can either sanctify all of life or destroy it all for what we want and they want me dead and I can't move they have the power I'm going to die maybe I should stop whining because I mean sure all of that is true enough but so few people bother to try to truly understand the world and understanding the world is necessary for morality I think I have to pee does having to pee keep you warm when it is cold or does it expend too much energy having to maintain the temperature of extra liquid which gets cold burns more calories and you die quicker and where was I what about the people when are they coming back? they're just going to kill me why not do it now get it over with this is miserable and no way to treat a person I bet they don't even know I'm conscious! if they did there would be no way this is legal could be legal at all no! no person should suffer like this ever not ever no sir I honestly now wish I were dead knowing that my death is impending as it is I can feel a really weird need to shiver this table and this room is so cold but I can't do it and its weird because that should be instinctive but I can't my computer has been overridden all because these people fucked up filling me with some sedative and yet these are the people that get to determine who lives and dies? actually technically no because the people who are killing me are probably doctors and all educated and trained and the people who really truly killed me who sentenced me and condemned me to death to this fate if only they knew what they have done they are probably all a bunch of uneducated idiots who think all murderers should be executed because that's how society works besides if I had knowingly killed Mary I would have confessed and requested execution because I don't deserve to live but I wasn't even me at the trial and yet they sentenced me to death without even giving me a chance to speak well I guess they technically gave me a chance but not really schizophrenics don't get to control their thoughts like sane people and now after ten years of the therapy they assigned me I am sane again just in time to die did they plan this? who am I?! was this their sick twisted intention all along? if so they deserve to be executed because this is the torture they prescribed in fact if someone condemns another to death and the death is torture like mine except maybe special cases where the crime was so bad even torture was befitting but then couldn't they be fixed through a long term endeavor on the part of society? possibly but I absolutely could have and they only let me be fixed so they could kill me the real me not the crazy me I was crazy that is such a weird sentence to utter implies insanity is only temporary which is so rare as rare as a flying turtle okay maybe not that rare that doesn't even exist but they're going to kill me because I'm not psychologically stable *was not* psychologically stable and yet the atrocity that I committed I would gladly spend the rest of my life in public repentance serving for the greater good in any way I could always well aware of my crime and what I did and would never fully atone for my misgiving do I not deserve that chance? if they could talk to me now if they could hear my thoughts they would have to be as insane as I was to condemn me again sure I could and should be killed if I ever had a mishap but what are the odds of someone with my history who did good as a kid and was forced into this no I did this stop blaming others you asshole! go back as a child and relive my life why can't I do that and just start over and find someone I truly like and who likes me ugh! at least I will die content with my thoughts as content as possible getting to come to terms with my fate like this wait what? are they coming in now? no! stop let me live! I repent! maybe not like the preacher said I can just live a good life and care for other people and forgive bad deeds and wrong doings that is what is truly good and killing adulterers and murders and especially adulterers is absurd just because they did something bad why would you kill an adulterer? why did I kill an adulterer? she was my fiancée I loved her she was my li—she was my lie I used her as a means to be normal I really did love her she didn't deserve to die! I was so wrong I

- 88 -

know that it is obvious I can't see is that them? why can't I turn my head? I hate this! oh fuck just stop whining and suffer just a little more sure this doesn't seem fair but maybe I am wrong and besides the next drugs are going to kill me and it will all be over before I ever realize it just dark empty nothingness the weirdest sensation god this feels so weird my stomach is turning at the very thought nothingness it's so baffling I can't comprehend I understand the logic behind nonexistence but I will never grasp the feeling of such emptiness of void of gross ew! my stomach! oh there they are is that the vial? no don't please I don't want to die I don't want to die I don't want to die I don't want to die I don't want to die please just let me die! give me a bottle of scotch and a handgun and just let me do this myself in solitude as the sun rises something! dignity! just not this oh if only I knew the meaning of my life was why am I asking such grandiose questions as I die? shouldn't I have asked these of myself much earlier? would I have answered them before I ever died? does it matter? did any of this matter? probably not it's all causal and this was inevitable no free will none of us have free will so why do we all operate under such a false pretense NO THEY'RE BRINGING THE NEEDLE! oh to circumnavigate causality with something as beautiful as true free will I would go back and live my life again and just be true to myself and admitting I was wrong maybe learning this is morality understanding the world is morality learning is morality but free will would imply that I would know what would happen next because I would know what I want to do I would just have to do it but no free will means so much I don't understand shapes my entire life before I am ever born I hope my death now as opposed to moments after it should occur doesn't negatively affect any lives I could never live with my wait I'll be dead FUCK! NO DON'T STICK THAT IN MY ARM! THIS CAN'T BE THE END! NOOOOOOOOOOOOOOOOO! STOP IT! PLEASE! I BEG OF YOU! PLEASE JUST LOOK ME IN THE EYE! MY EYES ARE STILL OPEN! NO! YES! MY EYES *ARE* OPEN! DON'T KILL ME! YES! STOP! STOP! YES! NO! DON'T CONTINUE! NOOOOOOOOOOOOOOOOO! PLEASE! OW! WHAT IS THIS GOING TO DO?! WILL IT HURT?! OH FUCK! CALM DOWN AND think okay I should be unconscious so this should just stop my heart and lungs or something and the worst I suppose is just the feeling of asphyxiation which would be horrible but maybe just maybe since I have come to terms as much as I can with my death I can get the briefest of moments of knowing the emptiness of death the closest thing to OW THE NEEDLE IS IN MY ARM! to oh god what was I saying? just finish this thought and your life is complete you can do this Joseph! ha what an irony! think come one you can do this oh yeah! I am going to get to be one of the lucky few to experience death to know death to *feel* death before I die no matter for how short a time it is wait is that? my my my my my MY VEINS BURN! AAAAAAHHHHHHHHH! MY VEINS BURN! MY CHEST! MY HEART! WHAT IS THIS?! IT'S BEATING SO FAST! I THOUGHT IT WAS SUPPOSED TO SLOW DOWN! THINK I'M HAVING A HEART ATTACK! I CAN'T BREATHE! WHAT THE FUCK IS GOING ON?! AAAAAAHHHHHHHHH! IT HURTS SO FUCKING MUCH! FUCK! FUCK! FUCK! FUCK! FUCK! FUCK! FUCK ME! STOP IT! PLEASE LET IT END! NOW! PLEASE!

THUMPTHUMPTHUMPTHUMPTHUMPTHUMPTHUMP MY
HEART HURTS! MY VEINS BURN! MY HEAD! IT'S DIZZY!
MY BODY! THIS IS DEATH! IS THIS DEATH?! THIS IS
DEATH! THIS ISN'T WHAT WAS SUPPOSED TO HAPPEN!
NOOOO! SO BRIGHT! JUST THINK! KEEP THINKING! JUST
KEEP CONSCIOUSNESS! COME ON JOSEPH! YOU CAN"

CHAPTER 8

The day after Joseph was executed, the man from behind the desk at the end of the corridor was due to give a presentation to a panel of authority figures from the prison and the community at large. He took his place behind the podium in the crowded room before an array of cameras, voice recorders, notepads, and inquiring minds.

"Hello all. As you all know by now, I am the psychologist who worked with Joseph during his stay here. I have here my official report to the prison and to the press on my findings in regards to the inmate Joseph.

"Are we all ready? Yes? Very good.

"Joseph was a conflicted man, particularly in a personal, introspective sense, but also a man dedicated to his studies and to finding truth in life. Unfortunately for Joseph, however, truth is hard to find.

"Joseph was plagued by several particular issues throughout his life, as are we all, but one constant theme emerged which ultimately proved responsible for his demise. He was a neurotic constantly in fear of, in reaction to, and subjected to judgment. Judgment by others and, as a consequence of his neurosis, self-judgment and self-pity.

"His life began in a small Balkan town where he was born to wealthy parents, parents who, in the fashion of their type, sent their son to a boarding school in the expectation that he would become a respectable man in his own right. This boarding school, however, would prove to be the location of many formative experiences in the life of the now deceased Joseph.

"I suppose, then, that I should begin in detail with his childhood. From the thousands of daily sessions I had with Joseph over the past decade, I uncovered one strong tendency in his youth; Joseph constantly longed for a sense of belonging and normalcy, for his place in the world.

"At first this insecurity of his developed as a byproduct of being a social outcast from a very young age. The other boys at the school were beginning to find themselves becoming young men and Joseph quickly found himself behind the curve. As a young boy he was a bit slow in his physical development and in developing sexual attractions. He felt panicked and to some degree less masculine. One particularly interesting story, divulged by Edna, whom I will explain momentarily, exemplifies this particularly well.

"One evening he and his classmates found a discarded bra thrown away on the outskirts of the campus. From my conversations with Edna, the personality correlated to this very event and this part of Joseph and his sexuality, I uncovered that Joseph almost impulsively grabbed the bra and ran, ran without really knowing why. He ran from his classmates until they quit pursuit and he could take privacy and hide away, until he could be all alone with his newfound trophy. With his curiosity aroused, he confusedly stripped naked and tried it on. Admiring himself in the mirror, his confusion only grew, turning into a guilt which he would carry for the remainder of his life. While there were no other such stories shared with me by Edna, I find it hard to believe that it was an isolated event. While it may very well be nothing more than a single, isolated incident, something which is actually not that uncommon among boys of that age, given the nature of his eventual schizophrenia and ultimate demise, I speculate the occurrence of other, possibly many, similar events. I was never able to uncover further instances of such behavior but I certainly expect that they occurred. Nevertheless, in all likelihood his self-perceived sexuality had become perfectly equivocal. Indeed my justification for this belief lies in the shared sexual experiences and flirtations of Edna while imprisoned. Now, Joseph was always in at least relative isolation here, so I am admittedly confused myself as to how any sexual encounters may have occurred, yet Edna readily shared them, implying that they were quite quotidian in both occur nature and occurrence.

"Nonetheless, Joseph shortly thereafter found his first, and only, partner. Her name was Mary and she was the victim of a brutal slaying by Joseph just more than a decade ago. They first met at a coeducational dance for the boys of Joseph's boarding school and the nearby female counterpart. Yet before detailing their relationship, and her murder, one more event from his formative years is needed.

"Shortly prior, Joseph had what appeared to be a definitive moment, one which had the potential to shape his sexuality for the rest of his life. He rescued a young homosexual boy from a vicious beating at the hands of some of his classmates. While he was never directly tormented or the target of homosexual slurs after his angelic intervention, he did become a bit of a social outcast, forced to find a new social faction within the boarding school.

"This new social faction was apparently quite accepting of Joseph, yet was understanding of the indifference which Joseph used as a rouse to hide his uncertainties and embarrassment, to hide himself from certain judgment from his peers. I postulate that it was then that Joseph began to more than question his sexuality."

The psychologist paused for a moment to take a sip of water from a glass behind the podium.

"And yet, at the most crucial of moments, at a coeducational dinner with the female boarding school within the same town, with a young girl who had heard of his heroic feat, of Joseph saving the homosexual boy from the brutal beating at the hands of his own schoolmates, Joseph found a female date to the upcoming dance. Joseph had been afraid of the dance, not wanting to attend and not wanting to find a date, but this young girl had pressured him into asking her to be his date. Likely only adding to the sexual confusion he was experiencing, Joseph doubtlessly found himself forced to reconsider the recent, sexually disorientating events. He again was forced to begin to come to terms with his newly discovered sexual preference. Being that case that he had never had any sexual experiences with another boy, no matter how much he may have longed to do so before he met Mary, Joseph rather quickly rid himself of what he probably rationalized as troubling homosexual desires. He found a sense of what he considered to be normalcy.

"This moment, perhaps the most critical in his life, was, in my best guess as a psychologist, the moment which defined his adult sexuality. His natural tendencies were still at best ambivalent, but his homosexuality was nevertheless undoubtedly more than latent. In fact, from what I perceive, there were definite traces of it throughout the rest of his life."

Again reaching for the glass of water at the podium, the psychologist smirked over the rim of the glass as he took the most miniscule of sips.

"As he and Mary grew up together, as boyfriend and girlfriend, Joseph never reverted to the aggressively anti-homosexual culture of his boarding school. That said, he was very much emotionally attracted to Mary and longed to establish a traditional family of his own; the thought of rearing children held a special allure in his eyes, for with it came normalcy. The attention she gave him was the most rewarding feeling of Joseph's young life; the love of another can be a powerful tool indeed. He admitted, or rather Estel admitted, again there shall be more on this later, that Joseph had found her attractive initially, though again I speculate not in an overtly sexual sense, rather his attraction mostly like stemmed from the fact that she once told him that he was an ideal man in regards to his actions.

"They became engaged immediately after his graduation from the university and began to live together straight away. Mary lived the life of an aristocratic housewife and Joseph took a job as an editor and a freelance writer. He was a deeply studious young man and had aspirations of becoming a great novelist. In fact, his school years after meeting Mary were predicated on intense study and even more intense delusion.

"His pursuit of some sort of universal literary theme which venerated the pages of the great works became all-encompassing. He began to shun conversation with his fiancée and his social obligations in favor of reclusive studying, studying which often kept him up into the early hours of the morning and thereby neglecting his fiancée sexually as well. Their relationship was disintegrating before his very eyes, and yet he was totally oblivious. And so Mary began to have an affair with another man, an old classmate of his who likely reminded him of the confusion once felt as a child and, as a probable consequence, brought yet more confusion and embarrassment.

"But here I should take the time to note that such academic eagerness is common among intellectually gifted young men in their early to mid-twenties, but, alas, so is schizophrenia. Around the age of twenty four, the age at which Joseph killed Mary mind you, is the most common age range at which schizophrenia develops, a disease more often attacking men than women, and with the particulars of his history, Joseph was a prime candidate all along. The mental illness kept him distant, in a constant pursuit of some literary truth, kept him working towards some masterpiece, kept him in fear of his first work being only the clichéd first work of an author intent upon not being a hack with great earnest, and, while his intentions may have been valiant in some sense, they kept driving him away from him his dear Mary.

"For those interested, I have here an excerpt of his which I found scribbled on the back of an instructional memo on submitting work for publication from a local newspaper company. It, to me, is perhaps a perfect encapsulation of the tortured mind that longs to do something great, something innovative, something particular, but knows also that what this is already been accomplished and thus never again can be. It is a perfect encapsulation of a person both fully aware of and entirely horrified by their fate, of a person who needs the attention they never got, of a person who fears more than anything else mediocrity, anonymity. It reads as follows:

> *'To be a novelist is not, at least not any longer, to attempt to depict anything in particular or to evoke any particular sensations or lack thereof; no, to be a novelist today is to have the perfect combination of ego and appreciation for the classics to want to leave such an imprint yourself. All depictions of anything relevant have been depicted, and all of the emotions which can possibly be felt by a human being have been forced into the experience of readers the world over, time over, by writers and by life itself. And this is not all. At this point it can seem that all that is left is to question is the foundation of the novel itself,*

but now even this has been done, done so well in fact that when people like myself think about the end of literature, even that is old news. The only thing left for a writer to do now is to complain, to complain that there is nothing for them to do. In so doing, perhaps ironically, though hopefully intentionally, they are creating something innovative, something worth creating; they are creating the next form of the novel.

As for the novel being dead, well, if I am right, then this shows that it can at least live on ephemerally, and without knowledge of the future all anything on this topic can ever amount to is speculation, but speculation is best served by a foundation in trend extrapolation, in probabilities, and the trend visible leads to the obvious assumption that, fitting of our pessimism and of our nihilism, those writers in the future will be at least every bit as bright as us, likely more intelligent, and certainly more informed, so why think that they cannot innovate further strictly because we cannot? Though, personally, I do hope the novel is dead. To rid the world of the pretension of the writer is to open the individual to the beauty of the sciences. To rid the world of the pretension of the writer is to give the world hope. To rid the world of the writer is to give myself undeserved validation. Damn do I want validation.

But we all want validation. That is why we all set out to become novelists. We understand, we think, quite a bit about the world in which we live; we have read and studied much on how it functions, how its components interact; we have learned what is the case, and we despise it. We then use the novel, and other like-minded media, to decry the status quo and affirm what OUGHT to be the case. We are nothing more than lazy philosophers who guise our pseudo-truths in flowery prose and metaphors. We SHOULD be genuine and explicit and communicate our sentiments with direct incitements. We ARE pretentious.

I want validation.

I want pity.'

"I would venture to say that these conclusions are indicative of that which underlined his schizophrenia. Without ever having had truly published any real literary work in his life, he had already begun to place himself astride the greatest, most belletristic minds humanity has ever been able to offer. Such grandiose visions, delusions, certainly became thresholds which determined the success or failure of his life, and while he likely often though it only a matter of time before his first 'masterpiece' emerged, he also was most undeniably aware of the preposterous nature of such claims, of the likelihood of his failure. And mind you that in his mind this is not simply his failure as a writer, but his failure as a human being. For how long before the murder he was schizophrenic, and to what degree at any given moment, we shall never know. But from there his intensive studies only exacerbated his delusions of grandeur and thus his first condition.

"First because his schizophrenia was definitely a contributing factor which led to the traumatic incident which, I believe, caused the onset of his second condition: multiple personality disorder. Mary finally broke the news to Joseph that she was having an affair, using pregnancy as a lie to hopefully validate her decision in his mind. But when she ran away to live with her new lover, Joseph, for lack of a better term, snapped. By being rejected he would likely have to relive all of the confusing and embarrassing memories from his childhood and the added embarrassment of his failure as a writer and man, something with which he had never truly came to terms or even truly acknowledged, so he rushed after Mary and murdered her and her new lover. But he did not stop there. No, the mutilation of his fiancée in an effort to find the fetus responsible for rending apart his sham of a life was despicable, but it did uncover one truth. There was no fetus and there was no pregnancy; Joseph found his former lover had been ovulating when he killed her. Knowing that she had lied to him, he realized that he had been lying to himself his entire life. Joseph was confronted with having to immediate reconcile the fact that his entire life was a lie, a farce of his own accord, that he could not achieve normalcy, that he was delusional.

"But knowing that his entire life was a lie was too much for Joseph to bear. His psyche split into four distinct personalities, one for each of the significant chapters of his life. The names of each personality were, after much study on my part and a review of the contents of Joseph's old bookshelf, determined to be the names of literary characters that Joseph knew and who loosely matched the foundational characteristic of each respective chapter of his life.

"Edna, attributable to Kate Chopin, was a strongly independent female character who desperately wanted to explore her own sexuality, much as Joseph did as a young boy. Later on, while in prison, Edna would try to fulfill these desires. This I mentioned earlier. Humbert, of *Lolita* fame, was a rather insipid personality, for he rarely emerged and offered little when he did, hence my categorization of this personality as potentially the most frightening to Joseph and thus the basis for most of my assumptions. Though I must admit that Humbert, rare as he was, never seemed to trouble Joseph while in prison. I can only guess that this was the personality with which Joseph least associated, the personality of which Joseph was most embarrassed.

"Joseph himself was the third of the four personalities, though perhaps an ironic mapping to the protagonist of one of Kafka's great works, what given the occurrences and outcome of his life. And finally there was Estel, a tough one to find on my end, being a pseudonym for Aragorn from *The Lord of the*

Rings, who was on a sacrificial quest to protect Joseph from his ultimate fate, even at the expense of much scrutiny and suffering. There was something which Estel was clearly trying to protect Joseph from. What it could be I can only speculate, but I think it unmistakably to be his past.

"When Joseph first arrived at the prison after his sentencing, Edna was the only personality exhibited. She immediately acknowledged that there were others, three in fact, thus confirming my ultimate conclusion. But she did not like them and wanted only to have the opportunity to explore her sexuality. Accordingly, Joseph's first few years were marred by instances of awkward flirtation with the prison guards whenever possible. But quickly enough Joseph, or Edna I should say, found each such encounter to be only an unreciprocated curiosity on her part. Edna admitted to me that she was embarrassed and avoided any further sexual encounters, claiming that the men of the community were deplorable scoundrels, and disappeared entirely. It was then that Estel and Humbert began to take more prominent roles.

"Humbert began to appear more frequently, typically when prompted by the visual stimulus of an attractive young girl, likely nothing more than reminders of Joseph's dear old Mary, but aside from a few mentions of embarrassment he felt about someone or something from his past, Estel began to dominate, coming back for good. With the weakening of Edna through the degradation of rejection at the hands of the prison guards, Estel was once again needed to protect Joseph from ever reaching the surface and having to deal with his ultimate anxiety. It was only after years of working with Estel that the first signs of Joseph finally began to emerge.

"First Edna returned, roughly one year before the execution date. Upon her return she was of a renewed vigor and excited to have the task of finding Joseph for me, though only once I had assured her that nobody remembered her past oddly enough. Estel, however, proved a veritable counterforce to every action I took. In the end, however, Edna seemed to have made much progress over that last year, for her actions were the direct cause of the revival of Joseph in the waning days before the execution.

"You see, I had subtly enforced and reinforced within Edna the fact that Joseph had a looming meeting with the priest. I never gave any further details, but from my talks with Joseph in between his final supper and his execution, when he awoke yesterday morning he was aware that he, Joseph, had a meeting with the priest, thanks, of course, to me and Edna.

"Fearing that I was running out of time and with benevolent intentions, I deliberately betrayed Estel, and the rules of the prison, by making Joseph's last dinner slightly different from what was requested by Estel, hoping to mimic the cuisine typical of the various phases of Joseph's life. In the end this tactic proved successful, for with each course, memories of that particular phase of Joseph's life came flooding back into his consciousness, forcing him to recall his true nature, who he truly was. My gambit was a success.

"Furthermore, after reviewing audio tapes from Joseph's jail cell from the week of the execution, I have determined that Joseph actually first came to the surface only yesterday, on the morning of the very day of his execution. The timing was impeccable, and for that I am grateful. Again I owe this very much to Edna, for she was my greatest tool in the struggle against Estel.

Nevertheless, when Joseph died, he died knowing the truth, and whether or not he ever wanted to hear the truth, whether or not it was right or wrong for him to hear the truth, whether or not one person has the right to interfere in the perception of reality of another, Joseph died aware of reality and able to pass judgment upon himself. Who in his position could ask for more than that? If only we could know what his last thoughts were, perhaps then we could know if his punishment was truly fitting. I for one would like to learn if the assumptions of Joseph's sexuality and their role in his ultimate downfall I made during my decade of work were correct. I for one would like to think he was once again honest with himself during his final moments, that maybe he found the truth that he was looking for all along. I for one hope that he never will be pitied."

With the presentation concluded, the audience applauded quite vociferously before leaving the room to go back about their lives, unaffected.

—fin—

Falling Run Press